TORTS

of the

SOUL

JERRY HANSON

ISBN 978-1-0980-2695-0 (paperback)
ISBN 978-1-0980-4194-6 (hardcover)
ISBN 978-1-0980-2696-7 (digital)

Christian Faith Publishing, Inc.
832 Park Avenue
Meadville, PA 16335
www.christianfaithpublishing.com

Printed in the United States of America

Table of Contents

DUCHESS 5

THE CAYUSE..25

ROGER..45

PRIVILEGED 61

PAWN TO BISHOP III..83

JACOB'S BUSINESS 115

HOWIE..129

CONSEQUENCES 145

FIGURES 169

BIG GAME 187

FAME..213

THE POLITICIANS..239

DUCHESS

I forgot to check into my flight twenty-four hours before departure. When I remembered and checked in, the only available free seat was a center seat in the last row. Begrudgingly, I paid the upgrade fee and selected a seat near a window and over the wing. The plane ride was almost over as we approached DFW-Fort Worth. My costly and personally selected window seat had not turned out so well. The seat was fine. The window was fine. My travel companions were not so fine.

Since I had paid an upgrade for my seat, I was allowed to board with the first group. I buckled in and began to watch the other passengers file down the aisle. I liked to watch them board. I guessed who might take the seats next to me. I avoided making direct eye contact as passengers approached my row. I am superstitious. I sometimes thought my eye contact could cause them to sit next to me. I purposefully avoided the faces of large people. They overflowed their seats. It would always be a nice surprise when a petite, nice-looking girl was assigned the adjacent seat. Not my luck today. Lumbering down the aisle came this large man. Surely he had played football somewhere. Maybe he even played professional football. He carried two bags that must have stretched the limits for allowable carry-ons. He forced the bags into an overhead compartment.

At a distance followed a large woman. I thought she might have played football too! She was not as tall as him, but she was just as wide. She was a block. Her hips were swishing both sides of the aisle as she waddled toward me. Seated passengers leaned in as she

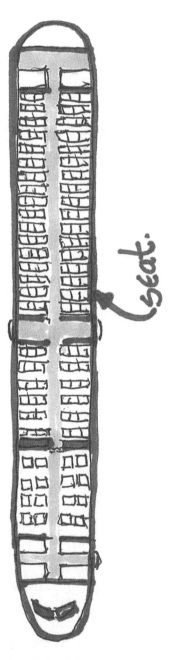

seat.

Airplane Seating Chart

ambled by. She was packing two large bags which ended up filling up and cramping my feet space. As they reached my row, I saw a medium-sized dog following behind. He was tethered to her arm. The dog wore an orange-colored vest.

Both presented broad grins indicating they were seated next to me. The man bent down and stuffed the woman's bags under the seats. Looking directly at me, she continued smiling as she leaned heavily on the back of a passenger's seat. She waited patiently in the aisle with the dog as he stowed the remaining bags. Boarding passengers were stacking up in the aisle behind her. Once the bags were stowed, he rose up, turned toward her, and said more as a command than a question, "Della, you want the center seat, right?"

She demurely responded, "Yes, I think that would be best with Duchess."

He moved away from our row so she could be seated. She handed him the leash and said, "Here, Deke, hold onto Duchess."

Clumsily Deke took the leash and tugged Duchess toward him. I watched Della prepare to sit. My assumption was she would sit down in the aisle seat and slide to the center seat. The center arm rest was raised when I seated. The aisle armrest was still down. My mental measurements told me she could not slide into the aisle seat unless the arm rest was raised. Della did not raise the arm rest. Instead she rotated in the aisle with her rump toward me. She made an upward body thrust. Her feet never left the floor, but her rump and body rolled upward in a fluid motion. When her buttocks reached a maximum height, she launched toward our seats. Indeed, her effort was a launch and not a seating. Whatever the effort, it was inadequate. The arm rest blocked her entry. She spun sideways, grabbing at the seats forward. For a moment, twisting and grabbing she clung to the back of the seats. Then she slid down. Della was lodged between our seats and the forward seats. She blurted, "Oh my!"

Her feet were in the aisle. Her rump was high centered on the arm rest, her stomach pressed against the back of the forward seats, and her head pointed at the floor as she faced the backs of the forward seats.

Della

Deke came forward with concern. His concern was not for Della. The woman and her child seated forward had been jostled by Della's lunge and plunge. They were jerked backward as Della grabbed their seat backs and then were tossed forward as she released her grip. Deke said, "Sorry folks." Followed by a quick demand to Della, "Get up!"

I wanted to laugh, but this was not the time or place. Della was stuck. Her size and awkward position were preventing her from rising. Deke leaned in attempting to grab Della's free arm. In the commotion, Duchess became excited and began to prance around. Her leash became wrapped around Deke's legs. He muttered, "Settle down, Duchess! I gotta help, Della!"

Deke half kicked at Duchess impatiently as Della tried to gain her composure and shift to a more comfortable position. She leaned on her lower arm and said, "Deke, give me a hand here!"

Passengers were stacking up in the aisle. Deke reached for Della's upper arm and gave it a tug. Nothing but Della's upper arm moved. Deke released Duchess's leash and straddled Della's legs in the aisle. He was about to attempt to pull Della up and out of her lodged position when a female stewardess arrived.

The stewardess hurriedly and sharply said, "Sir! Sir! Stop! Please do not pull on her. We will get her up! Just step back, sir!

Puzzled, Deke paused. He turned to the stewardess and said, "She's okay. I can pull her back onto her feet."

The stewardess responded, "I know you mean well, sir, but she may have hurt herself. We must take care. Now please allow us to do our jobs."

Deke stopped. He glanced at Della as she continued to flail her arm and said, "They are going to help you, Della. Just be still."

Deke un-straddled himself from Della and stepped back. The stewardess demanded passengers back up, so additional help could come down the aisle.

I didn't know what to do. I wanted to help Della. But what could I do? I was poorly positioned to physically do much. Maybe I could hold her head up. That might help. But I needed her permis-

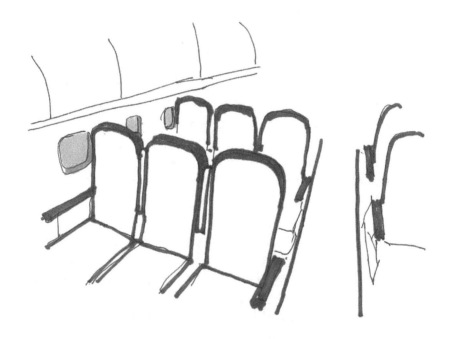

Seats and Arm Rests

sion to touch her. I am not a doctor, and we all know the legal system these days. Finally I said, "Are you hurt?"

Della responded, "No. I am embarrassed! If I wasn't so darned big, I could free myself!" She half-heartedly flailed again and added, "This is a fine mess!"

Deke suddenly bellowed, "Where is Duchess? My dog is gone! My dog is gone! Have you seen my dog?"

The stewardess immediately stopped directing passengers out of the aisle and said, "Sir! Sir! Do not worry about your dog. We will find her. Sit down!"

Two male stewards made their way around aisle passengers, toward us. They arrived and looked down at Della. They glanced at one another, and I noticed a smirk on their faces. They positioned themselves on each side of Della and said, "Ma'am, are you hurt?"

She said, "No, I am fine. I just can't get up."

They asked, "Does anything at all hurt."

Della said, "No."

The older steward directed, "Ma'am, my assistant is going to take your free arm and I am going to grasp your top leg. We will lift you up enough to get the arm rest out of the way. That is the first thing we will do. Is that okay with you?"

Della said, "Yes."

I queried the stewards, "Is there anything you would like me to do?"

The older steward said, "When we lift her, if need be, maybe you could support her head."

I removed my seat belt and readied both hands. The stewards kept the passenger backed up in the aisle. Deke headed toward the rear of the plane looking and whistling for Duchess. The stewards spread their feet and began to firmly ease Della from her predicament. I stayed alert in a ready position to help but did not touch Della. When the arm rest was visible, the steward holding Della's arm reached down to raise it. It was locked and would not move.

They gently let Della slide back into her lodged position.

Deke reappeared with Duchess. He said, "Can you believe it? I found Duchess in the bathroom licking the toilet seat."

Duchess

The older steward shook his head slightly and told Deke to find an empty seat for now. Deke did not obey. The steward summoned the stewardess from aisle patrol and explained to Della, "The arm rest was locked. We have help now to unlock it, but we need to raise you up again. Are you doing okay?"

Della replied, "My neck is stiffening."

The steward said, "Do you mind if your fellow passenger helps support your head and neck?"

Della responded, "Okay."

I positioned myself and locked my hands together under Della's head. My hands crushed her coiffed hairdo. She relaxed her neck. *"I wondered if all heads were this heavy?"* The stewards repeated their former process, and the arm rest was retracted. They let Della slide back into her lodged position to evaluate their next move. The older steward whispered to the stewardess to take Deke and Duchess to an empty seat and get them out of the way.

After some discussion, the older steward said, "Della, we are going to turn you so you are facing your seats. You will need to push up with your lower arm and we will use your legs to raise and twist your hips and body into position. From that position, we will be able to slide you face down onto your seats. After that, we will be able to get you up upright. Are you okay with that?"

Della said, "Yes, I just want to get out of here."

The stewardess accompanied Deke toward the rear of the plane.

On the count of three, I gently lifted Della's head, Della pushed upward with her lower arm, and the stewards lifted her legs and rotated her body. Della was still in her lodged position, but she was now facing the rear of the plane. She started breathing heavily and was looking disheveled. Her hair was now a mess, and her clothes were looking wrinkled. My manhandling of her hairdo did not help her look. I thought to myself, *Why do heavy people put so much effort into their hair?*

The older steward spoke very positively, directing his voice toward Della, "We about got it. Things are working well. How are you doing?"

Della dejectedly said, "Okay."

The steward said, "Our next effort will be to lift you up so you can slide face down onto your seats. From there, we can help you stand up. Tell me when you are ready."

Della took some deep breathes, waited for a moment, and then said, "Okay, I am ready."

The steward gave directions. "On three, again I will lift your legs and hips upward. Della, you will need to use your arms to push your torso upward. And you, sir," he said to me, "Will you help her lift up as much as you can?"

I responded, "Okay."

The steward counted to three and they lifted. The two stewards were able to use Della's legs to lift her hips and legs. Della was not strong enough to lift herself to the seat, and I had nothing to hold onto, so I did nothing. The effort failed.

I said, "I'm sorry I was not much help. I have nothing to hold onto, and I did not want to pull on her neck."

The steward said to Della, "Is it okay with you if our helper grabs onto your blouse so he can get a grip to help you up?"

Della softly and with out much zest said, "Yes."

I filled my hands with Della's blouse. The steward counted, and with great effort, we lifted Della high enough to slide her onto the seats. As we raised her up, I felt her blouse slackened and then become snug again, but it did not rip or tear.

Once on the seat, Della pushed up with her arms, looking straight at me. Her hair was a mess. Her lipstick was smeared. Her chiffon blouse was wide open with her front exposed. My lifting apparently shifted her blouse and popped the buttons off. Her arms in her sleeves must have provided support, because I knew I had been of help in the lifting.

I looked away and stammered, "I…I'm sorry about your blouse."

Oblivious to her blouse, lipstick, or hair, Della said nothing.

The steward said, "Just stay there a moment, Ma'am, catch your breath, compose yourself, and we will stand you up when you are ready."

Della complied with his directive. I began to feel sorry for Della.

We waited and the stewards stayed near. Della finally indicated she was going to stand up. The stewards jointly helped her right herself in the aisle. The stewardess immediately helped Della pull her blouse together. She reached into her uniform and produced two plastic airplane wing safety pins and secured Della's top. Deke came forward as the stewards helped Della sit down and slide to the center seat. Della's body spilled over into my space. The arm rest was still up and would not be coming down. When Deke sat down and slid sideways in his seat, Della moved even further into my space. I was now sitting in half of my costly upgraded seat next to the fuselage of the airplane. Deke motioned for Duchess to jump into his lap. Duchess complied and immediately walked onto Della's lap, looked at me, sniffed me, and licked my face. I was surprised Duchess could stand on Deke or Della's stomachs. I did not appreciate the face washing remembering Duchess's trip to the toilet, but smiled. The stewards left. Passengers were funneling by in the aisle headed toward their seats. On the way, Deke stopped the stewardess and made a request, "We need seat belt extensions."

The stewardess nodded and said, "Yes. Please wait until the other passengers are seated, and I will bring extensions."

Della had composed herself and said to me, "I hope you like animals? Duchess is very friendly and loves people. Of course, she has to be a very friendly dog to be in the pet service program."

I smiled and lied, as I responded, "Yes, she sure is a friendly dog."

Passengers were still filing down the aisle to their seats when the stewardess arrived with the seat belt extensions. She handed them to Deke. Our three seats overflowed with Deke, Della, Duchess, and myself. I occupied what seat space was left and hugged the wall of the plane. I couldn't help but wonder how this belt extension operation was going to come about.

Deke directed that Della would get her extension on, and he would assist her. Then he would do his belt extension. Della began to flail around trying to retrieve the seat belts she was sitting on. She asked me if I could retrieve the belt on my side, as she rotated her bottom upward. Duchess leaped over to Deke's lap. I gingerly stuck

JERRY HANSON

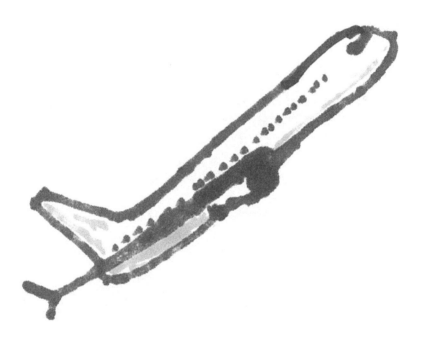

The Friendly Skies

my hand under Della and felt for the seat belt. I found it and tugged it gently from under her rump. She giggled and said, "I guess you got it?"

I said, Yup, I got it."

Deke reached across Della and handed me the extension. I hooked the extension into the seat belt and handed it to Della as she rotated back into my space. Deke helped Della and she was belted in. Duchess then jumped back on Della's lap with her rear feet in my lap. Duchess turned to watch Deke get fastened with her rear end and tail in my face. I avoided the view by turning my head toward the window. I softly cursed.

The plane was taxiing for takeoff, and Della started complaining to Deke that her snacks were in the bags beneath the seats. She fretted they could not retrieve them. Deke told her they could have the stewardess get them after we got airborne, or they could buy something if Della was hungry. This ameliorated Della. With Duchess's fidgeting hind legs on my lap, her rump in my face, and her front legs on Della's lap, we headed off into the friendly skies.

From somewhere magically, Della produced a stick of red lipstick. She meticulously began doctoring her lips. With her lips amply covered in red, she turned toward me and said, "My name is Della."

I smiled and said, "Hello."

Della continued, "My husband over here is Darrell, but we call him Deke."

Deke leaned forward, looked in my direction, nodded, smiled, and said, "Howdy."

Della continued, "I see you have already met our service dog, Duchess."

It has been my experience that most heavy large folks tend to be friendly, and Della and Deke were no exception. Della went on to explain Duchess was a Malamute. She is much smaller than most Malamutes. You can tell Malamutes by their bushy tails, sparkly eyes, and coloring. Duchess, because she was small, was allowed into the service dog program. That was why she wore an orange vest. Service dogs are supposed to be smaller, and Duchess was smaller when she graduated service school. But since school, Duchess had grown considerably.

In fact at her current size, Duchess could probably not be a service dog. She continued on how wonderful Duchess was for her and Deke.

Deke spoke up and said, "Nobody could dislike Duchess!"

Duchess, hearing her name, automatically wagged her tail, hung her tongue out of the side of her mouth, slobbered, and walked back and forth between myself, Della, and Deke. Duchess was a friendly dog and she loved her snacks. Deke reached into his shirt pocket and extracted a small dog biscuit. He hid the biscuit in his hand and waved his hand in front of Duchess's face several times and finally released the morsel. During Deke's tempting ritual, Duchess pranced her feet in Della's and my lap. In high gear, Duchess wagged her tail and exposed her rear. Deke, Della, and Duchess performed this little act no less than a half dozen times during our flight.

I tried to act like I was interested in the view out the plane window. I was not. I was irritated at my seat selection, especially since I had paid for an upgrade. I hugged the wall and tried to ignore my seat companions.

Della interjected, "I hope Duchess doesn't bother you? She is such a nice dog and just loves Deke."

I smiled and lied again, "No, Duchess is fine."

I muttered under my breath to myself, Duchess is a dumb animal. You two are the annoying ones!

Della began talking, "I need Duchess along when I fly, because I get kind of faint and Duchess seems to calm my nerves. When Deke was traveling with the football team, I used to go along. We did not have Duchess then, and unless I had a few cocktails, I would get sick to my stomach on the flights. I finally asked the team psychologist for some advice and she suggested a service dog! Wallah! We got Duchess!"

I responded, "Well, I bet you and Deke were happy for that little piece of advice."

Della responded, "Yes we were. Deke never took much stock in the psychologist until he realized how right she was about my flying with Duchess. We just love our Duchess to pieces, and you know she flies free. Being a service dog, we are allowed to board right after first class with the active uniformed Military. Actually, Duchess is supposed to be my service dog, but sometimes Deke boards with Duchess and saves our seats, and then I come just before they close the doors. Deke has no problems getting on with Duchess because he just limps a little bit and they say nothing. I like to eat and have a glass of wine before I board the plane and of course I have to finish it before boarding. Sometimes we travel with old football friends, and we will take Duchess with her service vest on to the front of the line, and the attendant will let us all board early! They are so nice about that!"

I said, "Yes, the airlines try to take care of their special passengers."

Deke said, "Hey, Della, tell him about Duchess last week in the supermarket. He will get a kick out of that story."

I knew I was going to hear this story whether I was interested or not.

Della began. "We go to Snyders supermarket. It is a very upscale grocery store. You know, a really fresh and clean produce section, a deli, a coffee bar, and a specialty butcher shop. Snyders has a sign that says, 'Absolutely no pets in the store,' but Duchess is a service dog, so by law she can enter. Well, Deke was telling the butcher how to cut some steaks for dinner, and I was talking to a stock boy not really paying much attention to Duchess. All of a sudden, the butcher flies around the counter and tries to grab Duchess from the meat display.

Duchess had pulled a full fillet strip from its wrapping and was eating it! When the butcher tried to grab Duchess, she growled and locked down on the steak. She must have thought the butcher was trying to take her food."

Deke chimed in, "Yeah, I thought it was funny. I know better than try to take meat away from Duchess. The butcher is lucky he didn't lose an arm! Duchess almost flunked service dog school because of her possessiveness of food."

Della smiled and continued, "Well, Duchess was growling and chomping on the fillet. The butcher did not know what to do. He said to us you need to get your dog away from the meat! Deke told him you can't sell the meat now, it's been chewed on by a dog!" The butcher left to get the manager.

Steak

Della continued, "Duchess had eaten more than half the steak when the manager appeared. We explained to the manager that we were waiting for the butcher to cut some steaks when Duchess helped herself to meat in the show case. Deke told him the meat case is at eye level for Duchess. That makes it very enticing for her or any other dog. The manager asked us to go to the front of the store and bring Duchess. The manager told the butcher to finish our steak order and come to check out stand number one. He also told him to have someone clean up the mess on the floor."

Della continued on, "Deke and I walked Duchess to the front of the store. Duchess was carrying the remaining steak in her mouth and waging her tail. Deke said Duchess is probably full and wants to go bury the rest of the fillet outside. We both laughed, but the manager just kept walking to the front of the store. The manager checked us out. The bill was for just the steaks we ordered. We paid for the steaks. The next time we went into Snyders, the meat case had been raised and glass covered the front. The price for steaks had gone up over thirty cents per pound."

Della said, "I think that was a good solution for the meat counter. They probably should have done that sooner. Anyway, now Duchess turns her nose up at hamburger! She likes steak!"

Della and Deke both laughed. I smiled and said, "That's nice. I am glad Duchess has found her taste in meats."

The plane hit some turbulence and the fasten seat belt sign came on. Della and Deke were both hard at work trying to re-buckle. They were having trouble with the extensions. As they struggled away with their seat belts, Duchess has prancing in my lap.

Della said, "Thank you so much for helping with Duchess. Some strangers she does not take well to. Like Deke said, she almost flunked service dog school."

I leaned against the wall and sunk back into what seat I had. I wondered: *How did all this service dog stuff get started?* These two bozos plow through life like they were still football heroes in High School. I recalled from my college days how the engineering and mathematics professors used to say, "Social sciences are not true sciences." It did not matter what the engineering or math professors thought or said. The university system rolled on. Social science was an easy, feel-good curricula with high enrollment numbers. In fact, the social science department had larger enrollments than the engineering or mathematics colleges combined. The psychology professors had PhDs just like the mathematics and engineering professors.

All professors used to do research and had to become published. Attempting to explain the universe or understand nature, the sciences and engineering always had problems to solve. They had been searching for truthful answers for thousands of years.

Contrarily, the psychologists, with little success, had been attempting to research human behavior and explain feelings for a few decades. For example, a psychology PhD candidate might get commissioned to do a graduate thesis on "nervous disorders of silly people." Some professor sponsored the candidate. The candidate submitted reams of paperwork requesting government grant funds. They organized a test group and attempted to measure calmness. Miraculously they noticed what we all automatically and instinctively knew. Pets and dogs, in particular, seemed to calm a fidgety soul. Other like-minded professors agreed with the methods and findings. A paper was published and made its way into *Trends in Psychology*. A sports psychologist for a football team read the article. The football psychologist told Deke about service dogs. The next thing you knew, Della and Deke were boarding airplanes early, Duchess was eating steak, Snyders was modifying meat displays, and I was sitting here with a dogs rump in my face.

I hope this plane lands soon before I lose my calmness and need a service revolver!

I curled my body toward the fuselage and closed my eyes, just as I heard Deke say to Della, "Hey, Della, tell him about the time Duchess escaped us at O'Hare Airport."

"A man's insight gives him patience, and his virtue overlooks offenses." (Proverbs 19:11)

"Bear with each other and forgive complaints you may have, as I forgive you…" (Colossians 3:13)

Jerry Hanson. 2017

Doctorate of Psychology

THE CAYUSE

Rich Hardy stuck his shovel into the gravelly soil for the fortieth time and grunted. He was sixty-eight years old, and sweat covered his bald head and ran down his wrinkled brow into his eyes. In less than an hour, his cousin, Wanda, would deliver an urn holding her brother Donny's ashes to be placed into the hole Rich was trying to dig.

There was a reason the plots in the cemetery were free. It was completely overgrown with weeds, except where the deer had trampled on the grave site to eat the remains of flowers long past their purpose. Rich was digging on top of his Auntie Donna's grave. Wanda had emailed everyone that Donald Andre wanted no funeral, but Wanda insisted a ceremony be conducted as she honored his request to have his ashes buried with his mother.

The hole was nothing but gravel. As Rich dug, the hole widened. It was wider than it was deep. Wanda had asked any relative that could, to please dig the hole. In the Cayuse Valley, there were dozens of folks related to Wanda, Donny, and Rich, but none came forward. On the day Wanda proclaimed a ceremony for Donny, she bumped into Rich at a gas station and told him of her dilemma. Rich had not lived in the Cayuse for over ten years. Rich was on vacation and on his way to play golf. He took pity on Wanda's circumstance, did not show up for golf, went to the hardware store, bought a shovel, and was now moving dirt at the cemetery rather than the golf course.

As Rich dug away, he became aware of an odd feeling. He felt righteous. The original Cortese family consisted of seventeen chil-

Cayuse Grange Hall

dren. Each Cortese thereafter had no less than three children each, and 90 percent of them lived in the Cayuse. In fact, Donny had two brothers living in the Cayuse who may or may not attend Donny's ceremony. There was a deep feeling of family connection within the Cortese's, but they showed no kindness, helpfulness, or charity toward one another. Deep down, they felt proud to be a Cortese but could only show that feeling internally. Even Rich felt that way, and digging this hole for Wanda and Donny was the proper thing for a Cortese to do. Others would learn of Rich's good deed even though he would never mention such. Rich felt righteous.

Auntie Donna, the underlying occupant below Rich's hole, was one of the original seventeen Cortese kids. She was about in the middle of the litter. Donna had a crossed eye that looked sideways at her nose as the other eye looked forward. When she righted the crossed eye, the other eye looked at the other side of her nose. Donna was short but had a very curvy figure. Her most valued asset was a set of ample knockers. She flaunted her knockers and was well aware her eyes were not where the boys looked.

Donna went to the usual Friday night dance in the Cayuse at the Grange Hall when she was seventeen. Donna never drank, but she was fascinated by the "bad" boys who did. Fran Andre was at the dance and was helping himself to Gordon Smith's home brew. Fran was feeling cocky and self-assured and soon was fascinated by Donna's V-neck dress and her knockers as they jiggled and bounced while doing the jitter bug.

Fran asked Donna, "Do you want to try some home brew?"

Donna responded, "No, thank you, but I will come with you if you want to have some."

Fran and Donna went outside to the graveled parking lot, and from the back of Gordon's Model Tee, Fran extracted two bottles of home brew from under the rumble seat. Fran stuck the bottles in his baggy pants pockets and said to Donna, "We shouldn't be seen with the booze out here. Let's go out in the trees."

Donna followed Fran around to the back of the Grange Hall. They casually walked off into the trees. Far enough from the Grange Hall to not be seen but within earshot of the music, Fran opened one

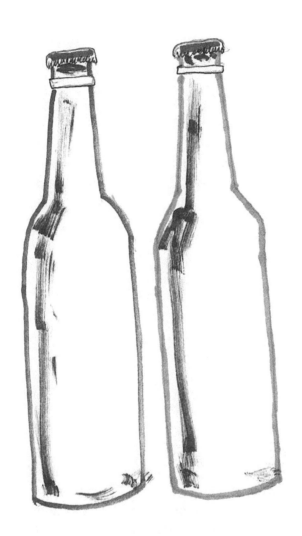

Home Brew

of the beers and said to Donna, "Are you sure you don't want to try this stuff? It's pretty good!"

Donna responded, "OK, I will try a taste."

Donna and Fran drank the home brew, and as they finished, Fran said, "I would like to kiss you."

Donna smiled demurely and came close to Fran. Their lips met very gently but lingered, and soon the kiss was deep and passionate. Fran pulled Donna tight against his body, and she did not resist. Donna was flattered and delighted at the attention never before paid to her and responded favorably to Fran's advances. The ritual progressed with fevered passion. Donna was a virgin and was awkward at times. Fran, on the other hand, had spent considerable time in the trees with young ladies. The encounter progressed to conclusion, leaving both Donna and Fran exhausted.

Fran carefully slid sideways to not put weight on Donna, and they snuggled together. Then Fran rose and reassembled his clothing.

Fran said to Donna, "Shall we see if Gordon has any more home brew in his Model Tee?"

Donna replied, "No, but thank you. You go on back to the dance. I will get myself together and come in a little later."

Fran asked, "Are you sure?"

Donna answered, "Yes, in fact, I would like it if you went in."

Fran replied, "OK, Donna, it was a great time!"

Donna lay on the ground looking up at the stars for what seemed a long time. She pulled herself together and began to slowly dress. Donna was peacefully happy but at the same time filled with guilt. She did not know Fran, except that he was a good-looking Frenchman who the ladies liked; he was also a good dancer. Donna did not go back into the Grange Hall to dance but walked slowly home in the moonlight. As she walked, she wondered what would become of her dalliance with Fran.

Six weeks passed, and Donna missed her second cycle. She later found out that she was pregnant with Fran's baby. The Cortese's were a religious clan, and out-of-wedlock pregnancies were frowned upon. But Donna would never consider aborting the baby. It was only six weeks before her senior year ended, and she would graduate from high school. She thought, after graduation, maybe she could move out of the Cayuse and have her baby. Donna was an emotional mess. She was happy inside but riddled with guilt and worried about her parents' judgment and how she would appear to her high school friends.

At the gas station one day, Donna saw Fran. She had girded herself to be a mature adult about her circumstance and had her plan to leave town, get a job, and have her baby. With determination, Donna approached Fran without intimidation or fear.

Donna said, "Hello, Fran. Do you remember me?"

Fran replied, "I sure do, Donna. I was thinking about getting in contact with you."

Donna cut to the chase and said, "Fran, I am pregnant."

Fran stopped pumping gas and looked down. He slowly said, "What do you want to do?'

Donna answered, "I am about two months along. School ends May fifth, the day after my birthday. I will celebrate my birthday and graduation with my family and then leave town, find a job, and have my baby. That's what I have decided to do."

Fran said, "Well, what then? Are you going to keep the baby and raise it?"

Donna exclaimed, "Of course, I am, Fran!"

Fran said, "I want to help you. We can get married. If you don't want to marry, I can move with you anyway, work, and give you money. This is not all on you, Donna."

Donna was relieved to hear what Fran had to say. It made her feel not so alone. She responded, "Thank you, Fran, for being a gentleman. I have to tell my parents of my situation and plan. I am afraid of the outfall and have not found the courage to approach them. I am afraid I have disappointed them to our family, their friends, and church community."

Donna could not help herself and began to cry. Fran stopped pumping gas, moved next to Donna, hugged her, and told her, "Everything is going to be OK."

When Donna recovered, Fran said, "We will tell your parents together, and then we will get married. I have a good job logging, and we can get by. What do you say?"

Through tear-filled eyes, Donna squeaked, "Thank you, Fran. You make me so happy to not be all alone."

Donna and Fran met with Mr. and Mrs. Cortese and told them of the pregnancy and their plan. The Cortese's were shocked at first and asked many questions including financial support and where would they live. Not once did they question if Donna and Fran loved one another.

A decision was made. Donna would finish high school. Fran would keep working and try to find a winter job. The week after graduation, Mr. and Mrs. Cortese would accompany Donna and Fran across the state line, obtain a proper marriage license, and they would be married. Nothing would be said in the community, and Donna and Fran would move in with the Cortese's.

The youngest Cortese was nine years old, and five Cortese children, including Donna, still lived at home. Fran and Donna would fix up the attic and use it as a bedroom. They could share the living space with the rest of the family.

A healthy and robust Fran Andre Junior was welcomed into the world. Donna was happy, and Fran worked hard at his timber job. The Cortese's did not drink alcohol, frowned on those who drank alcohol, and would never allow alcohol in their home. Fran liked to get home brew from Gordon Smith. He snuck it into the attic and shared it with Donna. They both would become light-headed which automatically lead to feverish sex.

One year to the day after Junior's birthday, Phillip Andre was born, and two years later, Donald Andre followed. Three kids in four years were crowding the attic. Then, Mr. Cortese died, and Mrs. Cortese insisted Fran and Donna move into the master bedroom. Mrs. Cortese took the opportunity to admonish Donna to stop having children.

Donna countered. "Mother, you and Father had seventeen kids!"

Burning Cortese House

Although Donna did not like the situation, the three boys played and slept in the attic. Junior and Phillip were easy going and got along well together. Donald was different. He was high-strung, full of energy, sneaky, and Donna did not discipline him or rule him in. Junior and Phillip stayed away from Donald whenever possible. Otherwise, they were in constant trouble with Donna for doing something to Donald. Donald was a notorious tattler on top his bad behavior.

When Donald was five years old, the boys were playing before bedtime in the attic. It was a dark winter evening, and a kerosene lantern was lit for light and a little heat in the attic. Junior and Phillip were playing a card game, and Donald was messing up their cards. Phillip pushed Donald and told him to stop! Donald went to the top of the steep attic ladder, picked up the kerosene lantern, and threw it on the floor toward the card game. The lamp broke, spilling kerosene across the floor, into the card game, and down the ladder. Donald shot down the ladder into the living room. Flames immediately shot up, catching the scatter rug on fire as well as the shear curtains at the top of the ladder. Junior and Phillip were trapped behind the flames.

Donald yelled to Donna that the lamp had tipped over and there was a fire. Donna fought through the flames to the scared boys huddling against their fiery bed. She smashed the window out of the attic gable and pushed the boys onto the roof into the cold snowy evening. Donna crawled onto the roof. The other Cortese children and Mrs. Cortese leaned a ladder against the roof to get the boys and Donna off the roof. Both boys suffered severe facial and arm burns. Phillip had been severely cut on the glass, going through the window. The whole attic was in flames, and the Cortese's and Andres watch the homestead house burn to the ground.

The neighbors took the Cortese's and Andres in while they all pitched in as a community to rebuild a large log home on the Cortese property. Various stories spread throughout the Cortese clan and the community regarding the cause of the fire. Donna heard two different versions from Phillip and Donald. Junior said nothing. Phillip insisted Donald purposefully caused the fire by throwing the lantern on the floor. Donald insisted the lantern fell off a small nightstand

Andre Homesite

because Phillip had pushed him into the stand and would not let him play the card game. Donna hugged Donald and assured him everything was OK. She told Phillip to stop telling stories and accept that the fire was an accident.

Phillip and Junior had pocked burn scars on their faces and forearms from the fire. Phillip's scars were more visible, and he had a jagged scar across his forehead from the window cut. The only medical attention given to the burns was applying a soothing salve from the Watkins Company. Doctors told Donna and Fran that the boys would be scarred for life. Nothing could be done to repair the skin, and it was unlikely the boys would grow out of the condition.

Feelings ran awry in the Cortese household, and, soon, Donna and Fran bought two acres off the corner of the Evan's farm. The acreage had a slow moving creek meandering through it and contained a pond. The land was cheap, and Fran, with help from the relatives and neighbors, quickly built a rough lumber house near the pond. The house was a very plain rectangle with four rooms. There was no money for siding, and the house always looked unfinished. When the spring runoff came, the pond flooded, and the driveway into the house became impassable. The water came up to the house foundation and ran under the house, but it never entered the house. The high water made their well useless, so Donna travelled three miles to fill fifty-gallon garbage cans with water from Thompson Creek for household use.

Two more children were born to Donna and Fran: Lavonne and Wanda. Wanda was the youngest. Times were tough for the Andres. Logging was becoming restricted, and Fran only worked part-time. He made his own home brew and began to drink heavily. Donna and Fran, when they were not having sex, fought terribly. The children tried to stay away as much as possible until Donna and Fran finally separated.

Junior took Fran's side in the separation, and Fran was able to get him a job felling timber. Phillip went his own way and got jobs here and there but managed to reside on his own. Donald stayed with Donna and continually comforted her and agreed that Fran was not a good father, a poor provider, drank too much, and was not a

Apple Pie

good husband. The younger girls lived with Donna and heard this dialogue repeatedly.

When Donald reached his senior year in high school, he got a job in town. It was difficult to go to school, perform his job, and travel into the country where Donna lived. Albert Cortese, Donna's oldest brother, and his wife, Vera, lived in town and let Donald live in their basement. This was a great help to Donald. Albert worked on the track crew for the railroad and sometimes was out of town for days.

One late evening after work, as Donald came in the porch door to head to the basement, Vera was in the kitchen.

Vera said; "Donald, Albert is out of town, and I have made a large apple pie. I can never eat it all. Would you like a piece?"

Donald had not eaten and in fact was hungry. He came in and took a chair as Vera served him a large slice of apple pie.

Donald sat where Uncle Albert usually sat and said, "Where did Uncle Albert get sent?"

Vera answered, "There was some track damage across the mountains, and his crew will be gone for probably a couple weeks. How are you, your mother, and the girls doing?"

Donald replied, "We do OK. Mom cooks at the Rustler Diner, and I give her my paycheck. We have a big garden, and during hunting season, the neighbors give us a couple deer. I guess we do all right."

That night, as Donald turned out the light and crawled into bed, he heard a noise and saw a light coming down the stairs. It was Vera in her bath robe, holding a flash light.

Vera said, "Donald, do you mind if I sleep down here? I do not like to sleep by myself and Albert is gone."

Donald looked up as Vera dropped her robe from her shoulders. She was naked. Vera was in her late forties but could pass for ten years younger. Donald was nervous but had become aroused. Vera turned off the light, slipped into bed next to Donald. As Vera hugged Donald, he prematurely finished.

Vera said, "That was awfully quick! Maybe we should try again tomorrow night."

Examination Books

She grabbed her robe and proceeded up the stairs to her own bedroom.

Donald was confused but elated and disappointed in his lack of knowledge and performance. Donald had never experienced anything like what happened with Vera. He simply could not believe it. Donald laid in bed and blankly stared at the ceiling in the dark. He was in the middle of finals at school but could not think of anything but Vera.

The next day, when school was over, Donald went to the gym and showered before going to work. He wanted to be clean when he got back to his room. Work dragged on and on, and Donald was inattentive to customers so much so, his boss wanted to know if he was feeling well. When work finished, Donald went into the bathroom and freshened himself again. He already had an uncontrollable bulge in his pants just thinking of getting home.

When Donald walked through the porch door, Vera once again said, "Donald, do you want another piece of my apple pie?"

Donald came into the kitchen, sat down, and answered, "Sure."

Vera served Donald a slice of apple pie, and as she bent over, he could clearly tell she wore no undergarments. He started to take a bite when Vera said, "Come on. Let's just go into my bedroom. You can eat your pie later."

Donald complied and followed Vera into the bedroom. She pulled the shades and disrobed. She was unashamed walking around naked. Donald clumsily undressed and crawled into bed. Vera followed.

She said, "Just relax, I will teach you what you need to know."

Donald experienced things he had never imagined in a relationship. Once again, he finished prematurely, but Vera kept him going. Their dalliance went on for nearly an hour when they both gave it up.

Vera said, "Donald, the goings on here must never be mentioned. You know how the clan and community are so pure acting. Now, why don't you go finish your pie while I clean up? Albert won't be home for another week."

Donald finished his pie, washed his plate and fork, put them in the cupboard, and sat down again at the table. He did not know what to do next or what to expect. Vera never came back to the kitchen, and after what seemed like an hour, Donald got up and went to his basement room. He did not study for his exams or complete his homework. He slept poorly that night tossing and turning, trying to deal mentally and emotionally with having a relationship with Uncle Albert's wife.

He left early in the morning for school and did poorly on his math final. For the next week every night after school, Vera invited Donald to her bedroom for extended activity.

Donald went to school on Mondays but did not work on Mondays. He stayed late into the afternoon trying to catch up his studies. Normally, on Mondays, he went to the country to be with Donna and the girls, but today, he would forgo that trip. Getting home at nearly five o'clock once again, Donald found himself in Vera's clutches in Uncle Albert's bedroom. As they lay naked on the sheets, the bedroom door opened. Without looking up, Albert sat down his suitcase and said, "I'm home early dear."

The room went completely silent as Albert looked at the couple on the bed. Vera sat up naked on the edge of the bed, as Donald clumsily fumbled to pull the sheet over himself.

Albert screamed at Donald. "Get out of my house, you ungrateful piece of crap! I never want to see you again!"

As Donald scrambled and stumbled from the bedroom with the sheet wrapped loosely around his lower body, Albert kicked him hard in the legs as he went past. He heard Albert say, "Vera, this is the last time! I have forgiven you twice before, but with my eighteen-year-old nephew! How could you? This is it! We are done! I am leaving you for good! You can go straight to hell, Vera!"

As the year passed, Donna took a job as the cook in a logging camp nearly one hundred miles away. The girls went with Donna and got special permission to be taught outside the school district. Donald graduated from high school with lower grades than usual on his final exams. He hung around the house near the pond and stayed at his job in town.

The community and clan knew something was amiss with Albert and Vera. Soon, rumors circulated that Donald was in the mix. Albert stopped making house payments and left for Alaska. Vera lost the house, rented a room, and found a job at a car dealership.

One day, after buying an older used car, Donald loaded up all his things and drove to the logging camp to see Donna and the girls. Donna told Donald she had heard the gossip about him but knew not a word could be true.

She said, "The Cayuse is so small-minded and cliquish, it is not a good place to live. Donald, why don't you get out of here and go to California? It's warm and progressive there. I'll never understand why your grandparents settled in the Cayuse."

Donald lazed around the logging camp for a week with nothing to do. He helped the girls with some math they were struggling with and asked if they ever heard from Junior and Phillip. They indicated they got a Christmas card but that was about it.

One day, Donald simply left for California. He got a job as the night clerk at a combination gas station and convenience store near the freeway. He held that job for forty years. Weekly, he telephoned Donna, wished her well, and told her how well he was doing in California. Lavonne found a nice young man and married. Donald rarely heard from her. Wanda stayed with Donna well into her thirties. Wanda was plain, shy, and very overweight. She did not inherit Donna's shape. She was much smaller on top, and her weight migrated to her buttocks and hips. She was poorly proportioned and had a terrible figure.

Donna met an older man who had a military disability retirement. He moved into the house by the pond, and Donna quit working. They raised a garden, canned vegetables, and hunted and fished together. Wanda hung around but got tired of being the third person in a two-person relationship. Donald invited her to come to California, and she did. Donald and Wanda shared an apartment, and both worked for several years. Donna's live-in friend died, and two months later, Donna died. They were both buried in the free cemetery in which Rich was now digging.

At Donna's funeral, all her children came to show their last respects. Junior and Phillip were standing near Donna's grave site when Donald approached them.

Donald said, "Howdy! Haven't seen you two for years? Have you missed me?"

As Donald neared, Junior watched him tentatively, but Phillip stepped forward and punched Donald hard in the face. Junior grabbed Phillip as Donald fell to the ground. Only a few folks saw what happened, and Junior moved Phillip to the foot of the grave site. Wanda rushed to Donald's side and helped him to his feet. Wanda and Donald moved to the head of the grave site, while Lavonne stood in the middle. They all stayed in these positions until the short ceremony was over. Nothing more was said, and they all went their separate ways.

Donna left the house, pond, creek, and acreage to Wanda as well as the proceeds of her live-in friend's life insurance policy. Wanda moved back to the Cayuse, lived in the house by the pond, and concealed the life insurance proceeds to successfully apply for welfare. Wanda lives there today.

When Donald died, Wanda had him cremated and the urn shipped to the Cayuse. She notified all the clan and the community of Donald's passing, his wish to have his ashes buried with his mother, and requested a family member dig the hole for Donald's urn. Rich was the only relative to respond to her request.

Wanda drove up to the cemetery in an old car. She got out and waddled toward Donna's grave site. Wanda nodded to Rich and said, "Hi, Rich! It sure is hot out here."

Rich replied, "I think I got this hole as deep as we can go. When do you want to start your ceremony?"

Wanda said, "I never heard back from anyone but you, Rich. I don't know if anyone will come. I'll sit down here for a while and see if anyone comes."

Rich responded, "OK. And they waited for nearly an hour. No one came.

"Let's go ahead and do this thing for Donald. Do you want to say anything, Rich?" Wanda said.

Rich was caught off guard and muttered, "Uh, OK. Uh, sure." He then mumbled a partial and unintelligible rendition of the Lord's Prayer.

Wanda said, "God bless you, Donald. I know you can now be with Mother, and no one can judge or criticize you any longer!"

Rich walked over into the shade of the trees, giving Wanda some private time at the grave site. Finally, Wanda nodded to Rich and waddled back down to her car. She drove off. Rich took the shovel and covered the urn. He said a silent prayer for both Donald and his Auntie Donna as he neatly topped off the hole and tenderly placed the cut flowers Wanda had left.

Rich arose and looked at his new shovel. He had no further need for the shovel and leaned it against a tree. He headed for his car. He felt good about himself. Rich guessed he had done a fine thing and not just for himself this time. He knew Donna's sister, his late mother, would be pleased with him. He started his car and headed for the golf course to make arrangements for one last round of golf before he left the Cayuse.

"...remember you cannot ignore God...a man will always reap the kind of crop he sows!"
(Galatians 6:7)

Jerry Hanson. 2019

ROGER

All the pleasures and nice amenities of life, afforded Roger, came from the efforts of others. His parents, family, and even friends gave him things. Roger had this innate ability of letting others know what he wanted, without asking. He acted ever so humble, yet he was never really grateful. He mastered how to dispatch false gratefulness. He was easily satisfied because all his wants were material in nature. Anything of interest to him could be purchased with money. He liked cars, fine dining, movies, the theater, sporting events, and golf and polo. Roger's world was sated by anything money could buy.

Roger's second vice was receiving attention. He loved being important. The more people surrounding Roger the better. He referred to all the people around him as his friends. They were not his friends. At best they were acquaintances. They were shallow, self-centered, and arrogant, just like Roger. He quickly learned the more money he had and the more money he spent, the more people liked to hang around him.

Being popular and having money was the perfect life for Roger. Roger's car and money enabled him to date three separate girls simultaneously. He made sure each girl lived in separate parts of town, and he was very careful they did not mingle socially. He juggled his time with each. All three girls were pretty, loved to go out, let Roger spend money on them, and continually focused their attention on Roger. Roger did not love the girls; he loved the attention.

Money

Roger did not know it, but he actually had a good friend, Ben. Roger and Ben had known one another for years. They met in third grade. Ben and his family lived on the lessor side of town. Ben's father and mother held menial jobs and often were out of work. Ben was a very good athlete, a far better athlete than Roger could ever hope to be. Roger hung around Ben at athletic events and loved to be seen with him around school and town. Ben's athletic feats garnered much attention, and often he was interviewed by the media. Roger would always be next to Ben when interviews occurred or when admiring crowds formed. Roger basked in Ben's glory.

Ben fell in love with the game of golf. With little effort, he quickly became a very good golfer. Other golfers were amazed at his ability and referred to him as "The Natural." Because of his financial situation, Ben had limited access to the local golf courses. His family couldn't afford a Country Club membership, and Ben could not afford the cost of continual green fees. Fortunately for Ben, Roger's family had a membership at the River Run Country Club. Although Roger only played golf occasionally, he liked to hang around River Run. Roger would pick Ben up and bring him to the Country Club. As Roger's guest, Ben could play unlimited golf. The golf pro picked up on Ben's natural ability as a golfer and liked to play rounds with him. Ben learned much about the game of golf from the pro. The pro encouraged Ben to pursue golf as a professional. He told Ben the best way to get into the pros was to get on a good college golf team.

Ben had never been on a high school golf team and had never played any tournament golf except at the River Run Country Club. He did not have the funds to afford college. He wanted a better life and agreed his best chance was to practice, play in some tournaments, and see if he could create enough interest to earn a golf scholarship. When he was not at his part-time job, he spent all his time around Roger and Roger's friends at River Run Country Club. The pro began to help Ben find golf tournaments to enter.

Ben was grateful to Roger and Roger's family. He was also as much in awe of Roger as Roger was of him. He continually complimented Roger, which Roger craved. Most of Ben's compliments were completely unearned and undeserved. He frequently in front

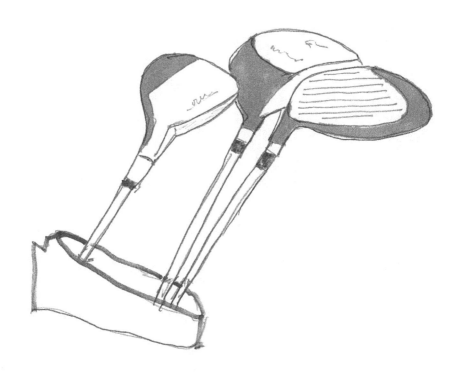

Golf Clubs

of Roger's friends said, "Roger, you got it all! A car! River Run! You are the luckiest guy! To top it off, you have three gorgeous girlfriends and they all like you!"

Ben had a solid physical build. He was not necessarily tall, but he was not short. He was not bulky, but he was not slight. On top of being extremely well coordinated, agile, and quick, he was well proportioned and muscular. Ben's athletic ability not only far surpassed Roger. He was also more handsome and manly. However, the girls seemed to be drawn to Roger more so than Ben. Apparently Roger's money, fun times, and the lifestyle were more appealing to the ladies.

Roger had money and he spent money. The more money he spent on the girls, the more they liked him. Roger knew the girls preferred him over Ben and other boys. He liked and did whatever he could to keep his advantage. He personally thought himself just as attractive as Ben. He knew he dressed better. He actually got better grades in school and thought his personality was fantastic. Roger just knew he had to be cool.

Roger's parents could not help but observe Roger's socialization and began to worry about him. They began to make comments to Roger which he considered criticism. They considered him immature. He demonstrated little motivation, held no known goals for the future, and his value system seemed to be void of good virtues. Roger's father thought he simply was not maturing into a responsible young adult. His mother often lamented that he seemed too materialistic and focused his attention too much on money and material things. They encouraged Roger to find more meaning in life and to put religion into his life. Roger ignored them. He thought them old fashioned, stuck in the past, not with the modern times, and way too uptight.

Roger's parents were socially liberal and fiscally conservative. Like all parents, they wanted the best for their son. Both diligently and dutifully went to work daily. They took their jobs and responsibilities seriously. They worked hard. They made sure all the bills were timely paid and provided everything for Roger including a generous allowance and car. They purposefully placed money in a fund specifically for Roger's college education.

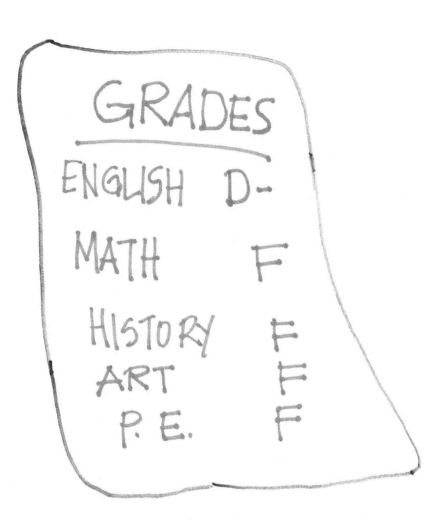

Grades

Roger's high school activity and academic career were mediocre and uneventful. He graduated somewhere in the middle of his class. He did not participate in any sports, played no musical instrument, nor engaged in any extracurricular school functions. Since his high school was accredited, all the graduates in the upper half of the class, upon application, were automatically accepted into state university. Roger went to state university. He soon learned high school classes were not at all like college courses. Roger couldn't game the college classroom like he had in high school. He had learned in high school that the teachers assessed your ability on your very first assignments. He purposefully got beginning good grades. He would then be placed into class groups where the subject matter digressed into discussions of eclectic subject matter, emotions, personal feelings, and views. Roger mastered the art of "bull shitting" his way through courses.

At State, by midterms of the first semester, Roger had earned four solid Fs and one D. Upon completion of the semester, he was placed on academic probation for poor grades. He was not a gifted academic student, but he would not be considered dumb. He lacked motivation and was lazy. Daily he slept in until nearly noon. He missed most of his classes. Even in the afternoons when he should be in class, he chose to hang around the student union building and anywhere else there was a group or a party. He invited his hometown girl friends to come visit and stay with him over the weekends. He developed a few other girlfriend relationships at college.

Roger intercepted college grade reports and letters sent to his parents. He simply changed their address to his off campus house address. He doctored test results and grades sheets to send to his parents on university stationery and envelopes. Roger frequently and openly lied to his parents about school. He convinced them he was in an advanced study program leading to graduation in three years with automatic placement into graduate school. His parents were very proud. On visits home, Roger used his girlfriends to validate his academic claims.

At the end of the second semester, Roger was expelled from state university for failure to perform to an academic standard. In two semesters, he had a grade point average below 1.0. However, he

JERRY HANSON

Parent's Buick

had made many friends. He captained a bowling team, skied, went on river rafting trips, and never missed a tailgate party. In fact, some of the best tailgate parties were thrown by him in his backyard. His social success and volume of acquaintances proved to him that his assessment of his parents was correct. They were out of touch with how the world of action operated. Roger loved the college life. He kept his rented house and made plans to stay the summer telling his parents he was working on a school project.

On one purposeful visit home, Roger convinced his parents that it would be easier for him to manage school and his finances if they turned his college fund over to him. As soon as they complied and arranged for Roger to manage the funds, he immediately indicated he had to return to campus for some special oral exams with his professors.

With access to his college funds, upon return to campus, Roger visited Universal Life and purchased a one-million-dollar policy on his parents. Roger explained they were elderly, and if they should pass away, his funding would be jeopardized. Roger made premium payments with his college funds. Roger shopped around and found and bought a Buick, the exact year and model his parents owned. While Roger's friends attended classes, he worked on the Buick. Spending time on the car made him feel worthwhile. The guys thought Roger manly and considered him knowledgeable in the field of auto mechanics. Guys and girls would routinely stop to talk as Roger loitered under the hood of the Buick. Roger liked the attention. Soon he was considered an expert on oil changes, spark plugs, replacing mufflers, power steering, repairing brakes, and performing numerous mechanical repairs. He expanded his large social circle even more by working on friends' cars and handing out free mechanical advice. He loved his social life, his expert mechanics life, and his college campus life.

Roger occasionally traveled home to visit his parents. He presented doctored grade reports and test results and gave glowing reports on his university studies. He told them he was given the Buick as a special project in engineering to enhance automotive advancements. He gloated about his new knowledge and adeptness at fixing or improving systems on cars. His parents were impressed and pleased with Roger. They were especially pleased when he changed the oil in their Buick and offered to perform some other maintenance chores on the car. Routinely on home visits, Roger would work on his parents' Buick.

Roger lived his life around the college campus calendar. On spring break, he went home to visit his parents. One Wednesday evening, his parents left the house to attend a Bible study. The Bible study was across town about twenty miles away. They took their Buick. They were running about ten minutes late, so Roger's father decided to take the old Highway 59 shortcut. In days past, Highway 59 was one of the main highways through town. The Interstate Highway System made Highway 59 a poorly maintained two-lane secondary route. The shortcut is a popular route for logging trucks even though it has a step grade. The loaded logging trucks slowed to a virtual crawl as they struggled to pull the uphill grade. However, the trucks on the downhill grade built up excessive speeds. After following a slow-moving truck up the grade for some time and running late to Bible study, Roger's father became impatient and frustrated. He moved the Buick into the opposing lane to pass. Traveling uphill, the Buick struggled to gain enough speed to overtake the truck. Concerned about oncoming truck traffic, Roger's father pushed the throttle to the floor for more speed. The Buick coughed, faltered, and did not respond. Roger's father decided he could not timely complete the pass. He chose to fall back into line behind the truck. He stepped on the brakes to slow, but they did not respond. As an oncoming empty logging truck bore down on the Buick, Roger's father swerved the car to claim his space behind the slow-moving uphill truck. His turning movement was too quick. He misjudged the proper time to reenter the lane. The front fender of the Buick clipped the rear end of the truck. The Buick spun around in the center of the road and was hit broadside by the oncoming downhill empty logging truck. The crash was fatal.

Roger's parents' estate was left to him. He got their house, what was left of his dwindling college fund, seventy thousand dollars from their savings account, and the proceeds of the one-million-dollar life insurance policy he had taken out on his parents. Roger liquidated everything his parent owned in his hometown. With his swollen bank account, he headed back to the college life. He purchased a very large estate home near campus with nine bedrooms and six bathrooms. He rented out rooms to college students and held parties continuously. He was very popular.

Due to a lack of funds, Ben did not attend college. He lived at home with his parents, worked part-time jobs to save all of his money, and continually practiced golf. The pro at River Run made it possible for Ben to practice and play whenever he wanted. He filled out numerous applications in hopes of getting a golf scholarship.

Roger continually pressured Ben to use his savings and move in with him at college. One day in a telephone discussion, Roger offered Ben one of the rooms in his house, rent-free. Another renter had left school and the room was empty. Ben had applied for a golf scholarship at the state university, but had never received a reply. Bored with his current circumstances and feeling he was not progressing forward in life, Ben accepted Roger's offer of free rent. He thought he could walk onto the golf team and earn a scholarship once the coach saw his ability firsthand.

Ben used his savings to enroll for a semester at state university. The fun began for Roger and Ben. It was like the good old days. Ben was his usual exciting self, except when he pouted about lack of progress in golf. The pouting ended once the partying started. From time to time, Ben and Roger dated the same girls, but Roger's money and spending always won the fair maidens' attention. Ben decided he needed a job so he would have spending money. Roger talked him out of a job. Roger confided he had lots of money and would be glad to help Ben out with a few bucks now and then.

Roger said, "You will make it big golfing, Ben, and you can pay me back then. You need to focus on your golf and be able to relax. With school and a job, you will not be able to focus, and we need time to party so you can relax."

Ben was weak and was always susceptible to the persuasive powers of Roger. Besides not charging Ben rent, Roger also began paying for Ben's share of the utilities. Ben was grateful and always thanked Roger and gave him compliments in front of others, but he also felt guilty about his dependence. When they went on dates together, Ben was at the mercy of Roger to pick up the bills. Of course, as usual, Roger looked solid to the ladies.

One day, Ben received a letter from a nearby small private college. The athletic department and golf coach, starting at the end of the month, offered Ben a full-ride golf scholarship. Ben was elated. He jumped with joy around the house and waited for Roger to return. Ben gleefully presented his good fortune to Roger. Roger was sullen, unenthusiastic, and glum.

Roger pouted and said, "Ben, be patient! You will make the golf team here at State. You are better than most of the other players."

Ben thought hard for a few days about Roger's plea. He had free rent and utilities here. Roger did treat him well and gave him spending money. Deep inside, Ben knew he could not depend and mooch off Roger forever. He also felt he was losing his self-dignity by not earning his own way. The golf scholarship was something he earned, and he would get free room and board plus free tuition and books. He decided, even after Roger's insistence to stay, that he would take the scholarship and transfer. Ben knew if he wanted to move forward with his life and possibly become a pro golfer, he needed to take this opportunity.

After a week of being rude and uncommunicative to Ben, Roger quit pouting. Almost suddenly Roger's attitude shifted and he seemed pleased for Ben and his new opportunity.

Roger said, "Hey, this is great, Ben! We aren't that far away. I can come over to your place, and on weekends and big games, you can come here. We can still party! You can introduce me to some girls over there. It will be great! Besides, when you become a golf pro, I will be at your tournaments, and we will have access to the ladies!"

Ben responded, "You got it, buddy! I will make it to the pros, and we will go to tournaments together!"

Roger said, "Ben, you don't have a car. I got my eye on a new sports car that I have wanted for some time. I am going to give you

Ben's Buick

the Buick. I won't get much money for it, and it takes up parking around here. I will not take no for an answer. You will be helping me out."

Roger pulled the transfer papers together and arranged for a notary to come by the house. Ben was on his way to golf practice when Roger said, "Hey, Ben, you need to sign all these papers for me to transfer the Buick."

Ben said, "Can I do it tomorrow? I am kind of late."

Roger sad, "Just sign these two forms so the notary can do her thing. I will fill out the rest."

Ben complied. Roger took the paperwork to the Mother Vehicle Department and the Buick was transferred. On Roger's way home from the Department of Motor Vehicles, he stopped at Universal Life. With his notarized papers, Roger was able to purchase a large life insurance policy on Ben. He explained he was sponsoring Ben to become a professional golfer and needed the insurance policy to protect his investment.

Over the next two weeks, Roger worked extensively on the Buick. He worked on the brakes, the tire alignment and balance, the power steering, the transmission, and tuning and timing. He personally detailed the car. The coming weekend when Ben was scheduled to leave, Roger handed him the keys to the Buick. Ben was grateful and with tears in his eyes thanked Roger. They hugged.

Ben said, "Roger, you are the best friend ever."

Nearing noon, Ben headed off to his new school with the Buick. Late in the afternoon, the telephone rang. It was Ben's parents.

They told Roger, "Ben has been involved in a very serious and fiery automobile accident. He is in critical condition and not expected to live.

There was silence on the phone and then Roger said, "I am so sorry to hear this news. Please excuse me, but I must get off the phone before I break down."

Roger hung up. He sat down at the table and opened his desk calendar. He was looking for a note he had made which contained the phone number of a new catering service. The service not only provided draft keg beer and full backyard BBQ services;

they would also provide a small rock band. The homecoming game for State would be celebrated all week. Roger was going to throw the best tailgate party ever in his backyard. He dialed the caterer's number.

"They will betray their friends...puffed up
with pride and prefer good times to worship..."
(2 Timothy 3:4)

Jerry Hanson. 2018

PRIVILEGED

When you live inside a bubble, only the bubble affects you. We are all the same when it comes to bubbles. Some bubbles are much larger than others. Liz, formally named Elizabeth, was born into a small, uniform, and very stable bubble. As Liz aged, her bubble changed, some for the better and some for the worse. In some ways, Liz's bubble shrunk. In other ways it grew, but for the most part it simply shifted. At times, Liz's bubble was an irregular spheroid with bumps, bulges, and indentations. Life does that to all of us. Usually, those who are more stable and well adjusted have a smoother more uniform bubble in which to function.

Liz was the middle girl of Edward and Cynthia Drake. Cynthia would never go by the shortened name of Cindy. It annoyed her that her daughters all had nicknames. The Drakes lived in rural Dole, California. Dole was the county seat. The Chrysler dealership was the largest private business in Dole. Edward, whom everyone except Cynthia called Eddie, was a salesman at the dealership which Cynthia's family, the Dentons, had owned for two generations. The Dentons and likewise the Drakes would never consider owning a Ford or Chevrolet. Heaven forbid they would ever sell them!

Cynthia was not a pretty or graceful woman, and most folks in Dole figured Eddie had married Cynthia for social status and the dealership. Eddie was small, athletic, and good looking by Dole standards. Eddie played the gentleman role when necessary, was amiable,

Denton Chrysler

and well liked. He was fashionable and dressed immaculately. Most thought Eddie fastidious and a little too neat.

Kathryn was Elizabeth's older sister. Kathryn went by the name Kate. Kate and Liz shared similar looks and stature. Unfortunately for them, they resembled Cynthia more than Eddie. The younger sister, Susanne, known as Suzy, looked and acted more like Eddie. Liz not only got the worst of Cynthia's looks and matronly size, she also relied fully on family status and family name for recognition and popularity. Through grammar school in Dole, things went well for Liz. Her group of girlfriends took piano, dance, and gymnastic classes together. They shopped at the more upscale Dole Mercantile and went on family ski vacations together. Their parents were politically active. They knew the mayor, state assemblyman, and superintendent of schools on a personal basis.

Cynthia's parents passed away within a two-month period, and she became the sole owner of Denton Chrysler. She gave Eddie full responsibility to manage and run the business. It was a mistake. Eddie was not a good manager nor a good businessman. Eddie was simply a good salesman. Cynthia spent her afternoons hosting bridge parties, political fund-raisers, and drinking wine with the proper women of Dole. To assure political correctness, she hosted a monthly Bible study in her home. The Chrysler business was failing under Eddie's management. Eddie focused business efforts on inviting special guests and his favored salesmen and women on duck hunting outings. They stayed at a favorite hunting lodge, and the Denton Motor Company picked up the tab. Cynthia's father had sponsored these same junkets to promote business for years. Cynthia thought the outings were simply part of normal business.

Julian Barns was the mayor of Dole. Julian was also president of First Bank of Dole. Over a home-cooked evening meal, Julian mentioned to his wife, Yolanda, that the Denton Motor Company was getting further and further behind with their monthly debt payments. The mayor was concerned since Eddie Drake rarely came into the bank. Cynthia Denton Drake had plenty of assets to back up their line of credit, but the debt had grown to over one million dollars. Yolanda, attending the weekly bridge gathering at Cynthia's, felt it was her duty to whisper the mayor's concerns about the dealership to Cynthia. Cynthia took the news in stride and stated, "I'm sure Eddie has control of the situation."

Cynthia knew if Yolanda Barns had a secret, every important person in Dole knew the secret. On Monday morning, Cynthia went downtown to visit Bert Claymore. Bert was a long-time Denton family friend. Bert had prepared the Denton family taxes for years. He also was the managing trustee of the Denton Family Trust. Cynthia unquestionably trusted Bert, and she relayed Yolanda's comments regarding the dealership.

Bert responded, "Yes, Cynthia, I have heard the same comments around Dole." He continued, "Cynthia, with your permission, I think we should quietly check out the dealership and perform an audit. What do you think?"

Cynthia thought for a moment and then replied, "Bert, you would be very proper about this and do nothing to make Eddie look foolish or become suspicious."

Bert said, "Of course, Cynthia, we are on the same page about this little matter."

Over the next month, Bert quietly audited the operations, management, and finances of the Denton Motor Company. Bert told Eddie the audit had to be performed for the trust. Eddie paid scant attention to the finances of the business and thought nothing of Bert's work. Eddie made the dealership open for full review to Bert and his staff. With the audit complete, Bert made arrangements for Cynthia to come to his office. He asked Cynthia to take a seat, offered her a soft drink, and reported.

Bert said, "Cynthia, the Denton Motor Company has lost money every year since your father passed away. First Bank is owed over one million dollars, and if all payables were included, the dealership would be in debt over two million dollars. Cynthia, you may find this uncomfortable, but I must tell you the truth. Eddie may be a good person, but he is inept as a businessman. To his demise, Eddie wants to be everybody's friend. He is well liked, but being liked can be a detriment at times and does not necessarily lead to being a good businessman. You must know Eddie loves to party and he probably drinks too much."

Cynthia responded, "Well, Bert, Eddie spends a lot of time at work, and I know he must feel the pressure of taking father's place. I know he cares about the business, myself, and the girls."

Bert replied, "I know, Cynthia, and I like Eddie, but as a long-time family confidant and family friend, and your personal friend, I must be completely honest and open with you."

Bert leaned forward and looked at Cynthia over his spectacles. For the first time in their meetings, Cynthia appeared concerned. She had not touched her beverage. She leaned forward in her chair, sat stiff backed and upright, and firmly grasped her purse.

Bert dropped his eyes to his desk, cleared his throat, and returned his gaze to Cynthia. Their eyes met. Bert said, "Cynthia, Eddie is having an affair. He has had numerous affairs with the women in the office, the sales force, and even customers."

Cynthia's position did not change. She stared vacantly at Bert. Finally she asked, "Has Eddie completely squandered my wealth?"

Bert said, "No, not yet. You have your parents' house, the one hundred acres, and the four commercial buildings they left you, and the trust that I manage on your behalf has nearly three million dollars. However, I suggest you sell the dealership before it becomes less valuable and pay off all the debt as soon as possible."

Cynthia looked intently at Bert and said, "Thank you, Bert, for being square with me. I appreciate your honesty."

Cynthia stood up, shook Bert's hand, and promptly left his office. On the way home, she went by the dealership and without knocking entered Eddie's spacious corner office. Eddie was sitting behind his large mahogany desk. A middle-aged woman was sitting on his lap. Her blouse was open and her bra was down. Eddie was giggling and fondling the woman. Startled, the woman jumped up, pulled her blouse together, and quickly scurried from the room.

Eddie looked down at his desk as Cynthia turned and promptly left his office.

Eddie came home late in the evening with liquor on his breath. Cynthia had waited supper and the family sat down to dine. Cynthia

The Drake's House

started passing food around the table. She made small talk with the girls about school and the weather.

Then Cynthia firmly stated, "I am selling the dealership as soon as possible."

Eddie retorted, "Cynthia, we all need to discuss this. We should not do anything in haste. I have made some mistakes, but all that can be fixed. This is too drastic of a reaction!"

Liz's bubble was bursting as the discussion continued and turned toward arguing. She asked herself, *What will I do if they move? All my friends? All my activities?*

Cynthia adamantly stated, "Father and Mother left me this business and you have mismanaged it! We are in debt and losing money. My reputation in Dole is ruined! I am directing Bert to get the best offers he can and sell everything we own here in Dole. The girls and I will move. My cousin lives in Astoria and we may move there. We will discuss the move later, but my decision is final on this matter!"

Cynthia left the table and the room. Kate and Suzy quietly began to clear the table and do the dishes. Liz followed Eddie into the parlor and sat on the couch near him.

Liz said, "Daddy, what are we going to do?"

Eddie replied, "I don't know, sugar. I think your mother is just upset. When she calms down, I will talk to her."

Liz said, "Yes, Daddy, please do that. Make her change her mind. I simply cannot leave Dole! My whole life is here!"

With stooped shoulders and eyes on the floor, Eddie slowly climbed the circular staircase to the master bedroom. Outside the bedroom door, his clothes and shoes laid in a disheveled pile. The door was locked. Eddie knocked softly, but there was no answer. He knocked louder and Cynthia responded, "Go away. I do not want talk to you! Go sleep in your office with your floozies!"

Eddie said, "Cynthia, I am sorry, but for the sake of the girls, we must sort this out."

There was no answer.

Eddie spent the next month sleeping in his office at the dealership. On Sundays, he spent the afternoon at the Drake house after the girls returned from church. Cynthia stayed at church doing odd jobs until Eddie departed the house.

The dealership was sold in June and a week later the house too. Cynthia's cousin lived in Astoria. With Christmas cards, they had kept in casual contact over the years. Her cousin helped Cynthia pick out a house on the right side of Astoria, in the best neighborhood, near the only high school and her church.

Eddie was purposefully excluded from the Dole selling arrangements and dejectedly hung around town. His salary was set to stop the end of August, and he had to figure out how he would live. He asked Cynthia several times to sit down and decide what they as a family should do. Cynthia resisted and avoided Eddie. While preparing for the move one day, it suddenly dawned on Cynthia that a custody case could be raised by Eddie.

Cynthia immediately sought out the bishop for advice. The bishop urged Cynthia to keep the Drake family together. He suggested Cynthia purchase a large house where Eddie could reside but live in a separate bedroom. Cynthia discussed finances with Bert and concluded it was better to use her family funds and house to moderately provide for Eddie, thereby avoiding public separation, divorce, or legal battles.

Cynthia silently opined, *"I have the girls, my church, my cousin, and I will make new friends in Astoria."*

Cynthia met with Eddie and explained what she was willing to do regarding their relationship, his family position, and the living arrangements. Cynthia's trust would own the house, manage the finances, and pay for the living cost for herself and the girls. Eddie could live in the house the same as before except he would sleep in his own bedroom. Eddie was to get a job and provide for his own clothing, car, and spending money. Cynthia explained it would appear to the community and the girls that she and Eddie had a normal marriage. They both would be civil and polite. With little input or recourse, Eddie as was his custom gave no resistance to Cynthia's proposition. The family moved to Astoria two weeks before school started. Kate would be a senior, Liz a freshman, and Suzy would attend the seventh grade. None of the children were happy to leave their environment, status, or friends in Dole.

Eddie landed a job selling cars at the Astoria Ford dealership. Kate began to hang out with a group of ugly but proper girls who liked to party. Their parties did not include boys but included pilfering wine from their homes or the church. They liked to go to the old steel bridge over the Astoria River and drink the wine. The most exciting part of the evening was to try and urinate, like boys, over the bridge railing into the Astoria River. That effort would end in much laughter, wet socks, and damp shoes. The group oddly felt special, since the water supply for the city was drawn a hundred yards downstream from the bridge. They thought their secret doings gave them some superior knowledge over the common citizens of Astoria.

Suzy clung to Cynthia and managed one friend from school. Liz loved and honored her mother but had a soft spot for her father's circumstance. Liz knew her mother and father slept in different bedrooms, but Liz never grasp the full effect of that arrangement. One night at a sleepover pajama party with her nerdy girlfriends, Liz happened to look out an upstairs window. It was well after midnight. She saw her father in front of the house across the street. Eddie was with the widow lady who lived there. They were drunk. They were laughing loudly and giggling ridiculously. They swayed awkwardly and bumped together. As they righted themselves, they kissed. Eddie grasped the widow with both hands and buried his fingers deep in her buttocks. He pulled her toward him. She giggled more. They proceeded up the sidewalk to the front door and disappeared into the house. That night, Eddie also disappeared from Liz's kind soft thoughts.

Liz was initiated into a group of girls at Astoria High School. The group was studious, well mannered in front of adults, liked by all teachers, and held all the school elected student offices. In the group, everyone made the honor roll, not by brains or talent to any great extent, but by hard work and study groups. They talked incessantly about boys and especially popular boys. A few boys came around them but soon departed for prettier and more exciting girls. Liz schemed incessantly with several of her pals about how to get certain cute or popular boys to invite them to dances. When prom

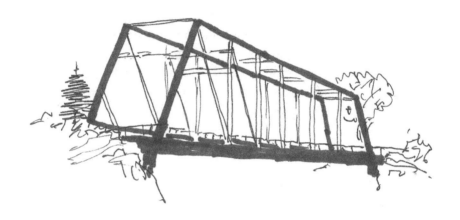

Astoria's Old Steel Bridge

approached, their efforts doubled. Their schemes usually worked for one date. A second date never followed.

Kenneth Garcia Junior had lived in Astoria all his life. From birth, he was known as Kenny. Kenny lived across the river on the lesser side of Astoria. Kenny's parents had been divorced since Kenny was a tot. Kenny lived with his mother. His mother drank a great deal and subsided on the welfare system. Kenny was gregarious, easily approached, and good looking. He was average in stature and a fair athlete. He was not studious but very fastidious about his appearance and clothes. He did not have a large wardrobe, but what he had was never tattered, dirty, or wrinkled. Kenny washed, starched, and pressed all his clothes himself. Kenny over the years had made one good friend, Rupert Duncan. Kenny and Rupert graduated from Astoria High three years ahead of Liz. With no job prospects and having flunked out of Astoria Community College, Kenny and Rupert joined the Air Force. They pooled their funds from Air Force pay and jointly financed a Thunderbird from the Astoria Ford dealership. Kenny and Rupert took turns driving and using the Thunderbird. Cruising in the Thunderbird, they spent all of their off duty time trying to get dates. The Astoria High School senior guys referred to Kenny and Rupert as losers. They continually and slowly circled the school in their Thunderbird to attract attention. One day, a couple of bold seniors shouted toward them at a traffic light, "You two losers would get more action sniffing bicycle seats!"

From the passenger seat, Rupert flipped them the finger as Kenny sped off.

One afternoon when circling the Thunderbird around Astoria High, Kenny noticed Liz Drake. She was walking home from school. Kenny, in his suave older way, pulled the Thunderbird alongside of Liz and said, "Those are mighty heavy books you are carrying."

Liz kept her eyes forward and kept walking, saying not a word.

Driving as slow as the Thunderbird could go, Kenny said, "I bought this new Thunderbird from a guy named Eddie over at the Ford dealership. Eddie said this cool rig would attract the ladies. Is Eddie wrong?"

Liz glanced at Kenny and said, "Was his name Eddie Drake?"

Kenny and Rupert's Thunderbird

Kenny responded, "Yeah, I don't know his last name, but he's a nice guy."

Liz said, "My parents raised me to not speak to strangers. Eddie is my father."

Kenny said, "Well there you have it. We both know your father and my name is Kenny. Now we are not strangers. We can talk!"

Kenny continued, "I can drive alongside you and we can talk, or you could put those heavy books in the back seat and I could drive you wherever you are going and we could talk."

Liz was atwitter with the attention. She slyly glanced at Kenny taking in his appearance and the new Thunderbird. She thought him good looking. Then she noticed two of her girlfriends watching this exchange from across the street.

Liz said, "Sure, I'll take a ride, but you must take me straight home," and she got into Kenny and Rupert's Thunderbird.

Kenny checked on Liz's pedigree, credentials, background, and status through his Astoria friends. He concluded Liz came from the right side of town, hung out with the rich families' kids, and got good marks in school. Kenny never thought Liz pretty, cute, or petite. She was as tall as Kenny and weighed fifteen pounds more than Kenny. To Kenny, Liz was adequate. She was better than anyone Kenny or Rupert had dated for more than three dates. Every Friday afternoon for the next month, Kenny left the base early and gave Liz a ride home from school in the Thunderbird. Liz's friends were giddy and quizzed Liz continuously about Kenny. On the fourth Friday after meeting Liz, Kenny took Liz for a milkshake at the Dairy Inn. He told Liz that on Monday, he reported for military deployment. It would be six years before Kenny and Liz would meet again.

Liz graduated with honors from Astoria High and, as was the custom, was admitted without exams to the major state university. Liz soon realized her and her high school girlfriends' dreams of becoming doctors or scientists would not materialize. Science and math were more than they could academically handle. University courses required more ability than going home every night and doing homework. The pace and amount of material covered were overwhelming. Liz switched curriculums and settled in as a C student.

After six years of sorority and school, Liz obtained a business degree and headed back to Astoria in hopes of landing a job even though she had no experience. On the way home from a meeting Cynthia had orchestrated for her with the chancellor of the community college, Liz was shocked when Kenny drove up beside her in his new Fairlane Ford. He said, "Hey, good lookin', how about a lift?"

Kenny was nearing thirty years old, and Liz was already twenty five. For the times, both were getting past the normal marrying age. Cynthia did not care for Kenny, and Suzy openly said Kenny was a twerp, "not worthy of a Drake girl." Eddie sold Kenny and Rupert the new Ford Fairlane. Eddie enjoyed Kenny, and every once in a while, they enjoyed a beer together at Sam's Tavern. Kenny used his military service to obtain a special hiring position at the Water District. After eighteen months on probation in his job, Kenny was hired by default as a technician. Kenny liked to lead people to believe that he was a supervisor in the planning and design department. Kenny was a junior technician. Liz was hired by the chancellor as one of four assistants. She worked on the fourth floor with an office view of an affluent neighborhood in Astoria.

Liz and Kenny dated, played co-ed softball in Liz's community college employee league, double dated with Rupert and his girlfriend Dorothy, and settled into life in Astoria. When Rupert and Dorothy announced they were to marry, Kenny and Liz followed suit. Cynthia was not happy but realized Liz had few opportunities and was aging. A large pretentious wedding was held in Cynthia's Astoria church.

Eddie sat near Cynthia after walking Liz down the aisle and presenting her to the bishop, the congregation, and Kenny. Eddie was sober and looked dapper in his tuxedo. Liz was pleased, happy, and impressed with her father. Cynthia could not help but notice how the older women looked at Eddie.

At the reception following the ceremony, Eddie began to drink, became loud, and dropped the drink ladle into the punch bowl. He snickered and reached into the bowl to retrieve the ladle. Cynthia, observing Eddie's behavior, actions, and his punch-stained tuxedo, asked the bishop to have someone escort Eddie home. Eddie did not go home. He went to Sam's Tavern. Arriving home in the early hours of the morning, Eddie found his belongings outside the door on the front porch. The doors were locked and Eddie had never been given a key.

Most families in those days had one income. Liz and Kenny had two incomes. They bought a house in a nicer suburb of Astoria and had a child whom they ignored yet spoiled. They settled into a rather dull life of jobs and socializing. Liz became consumed with the social interactions of community college life, hanging around the administrators and the instructors. She served on numerous committees. She never served as chairperson but was a dutiful participant, volunteer, and contributor. Liz was particularly involved in supporting and promoting the administration's implementation of all new government social programs in the schools.

Kate ran for and was elected to the city council. Liz fed Kate all the "goings on," wishes, and program needs of the college. Their connection benefited Liz, placing her in a position of influence and importance with the school executives, administrators, instructors' union, and other elected officials.

Liz's bubble was shifting considerably to the political left, but she, her sisters, and Cynthia insisted they were conservatives. Liz's university education, having never to work for her subsistence and hanging around government-sponsored programs, enforced her beliefs that government spending could remedy social ills, make up for perceived discretions, and fairly distribute the nation's wealth. Liz never understood or considered how these beliefs if they became policy could affect her. She also refused to recognize how clever individuals, on the dole, would take advantage of her and the well-intended programs she supported. As long as the lower levels of society did not live in Liz's neighborhood or affected her status, she was glad to provide free government programs. Liz, Kate, and Cynthia were quite happy with their status in Astoria. Eddie lost his job at the Ford dealership and moved to Nevada. Suzy married an Air Force officer and moved to Hawaii.

Kenny dutifully came home from his district job where he served as gopher to the engineers and administrators. He did not like his status or treatment at work, but he had few choices. He joined the union and with overtime was paid nearly what junior engineers made. He never got dirty at work and went to lunch only with the right people.

Liz attended meetings every night after school with various committees or with Kate went to board meetings. Since Liz made as much money as Kenny, she demanded the domestic home duties be equal. Kenny shopped for groceries, made dinner, picked up and delivered the children to school, did the ironing, and handled car and house maintenance. Liz did the laundry, the house cleaning, banking, and paying of the bills. Soon, Liz hired her mother's housekeeper and paid Bert's office to pay their bills, do the books, and prepare the taxes.

One evening their daughter Penny, was attending her music lesson, one car was in the garage, and Liz needed a ride to Tom Eastman's home. Tom was the deputy chancellor of the college and her boss. Tom and Liz were to meet the college chancellor at Tom's home. From there, the chancellor, Liz, and Tom would attend and jointly present a program at the board meeting.

Kenny drove Liz to the Eastmans and would go pick up the children later. Liz would catch a ride home from the board meeting with the chancellor. The Eastmans invited Liz and Kenny into their home to await the chancellor's arrival. Liz and Kenny exchanged pleasantries with Tom and his wife, Kathy. They accepted a glass of wine while awaiting the chancellor. A horn sounded outside, and Tom and Liz rushed out the door to their ride.

Kenny and Kathy were left to finish their wine. Kathy was a cute blonde, and soon Kenny found himself agreeing with Kathy's laments and complaints about how much time all these board meetings took.

Kathy asked, "Kenny, would you like more wine?"

Kenny said, "Sure, I have a couple hours before I pick up Penny."

Kathy went to the kitchen and discovered the wine bottle was nearly empty. She retrieved a fresh bottle from the pantry and began to remove the cork. It seemed difficult. The opener was flimsy and the cork did not budge. She walked into the living room and presented the bottle and opener to Kenny. Kenny reached for the bottle and pulled it and Kathy onto the couch. Kathy laughed but made no effort to rise. Kenny rolled her over on the couch, pulled her near him, and kissed her hard on the lips. Kathy responded, and the wine bottle rolled to the floor. In haste, with heavy breathing, the two groped one another. When it was over, Kenny sat up and pulled his pants on. Kathy laid on the couch. Kenny said, "Let's have that glass of wine!"

Kathy smiled demurely as Kenny extracted the cork, with ease. As they sipped wine they lamented about their marriages. They complained of all the meetings their spouses attended, the lack of excitement in their marriages, and their unfulfilled lives.

They finished their wine and Kenny said, "Kathy, you cutie pie, on Tuesdays, Liz goes to meetings at the school, I drop Penny off for music lessons at her friends, and I usually go play poker at the country club. How do your Tuesdays look between six thirty and nine?"

Kathy responded, "Tom is at those same meetings, and my Tuesdays are wide open."

Kenny said, "Well, let's get together. I can park on the side street and come to your house through the alley."

Kathy said, "Good, if the backdoor is ajar, the coast is clear. Just come on in."

Kenny and Kathy spent the balance of the spring semester with this arrangement. They enjoyed numerous rendezvous and activities. Kenny felt manly and fulfilled. Then, Tom took a job promotion and the Eastmans moved. The tryst ended. Kenny was glib and careful who he was around at social gatherings in case a country club member brought up the Tuesday evening poker games. Kenny had been playing poker but not at the country club.

Kenny changed. He became emboldened. At social gatherings, he was always on the lookout for friendly women, especially good-looking blondes. He would go out his way to be overly friendly and flirtatious to women while Liz continually talked shop and rubbed shoulders with administrators and politicians. Kenny's favorite greeting to other women was what appeared to be a very friendly smooch and a full chest hug that lasted too long. Some women pulled back from Kenny's greeting, but he persisted, always hoping for a friendly response.

Time passed and Kenny retired from the Water District with a pension nearly equal to his full-time salary. He had thirty years with the district. Kenny and Liz bought a view home on the best side of Astoria that overlooked the river. Kate's husband had died several years before and left her a large life insurance policy. Suzy died young of brain cancer, and Bert moved Cynthia with all her money into the best old folks home available. They learned Eddie had died in a rehab shelter in Nevada. Rupert became blind and lived in an assisted living center. Dorothy left Rupert for a doctor fifteen years earlier.

Kenny and Liz's daughter became pregnant out of wedlock. Liz and Kate secretively took her out of town to the best-known Planned Parenthood abortion clinic. She committed suicide one Tuesday evening in Kenny and Liz's nice home while they attended a political rally at the country club. Liz retired three years after Kenny but still worked part time at the community college and was active with Kate and the board.

Kenny, from his expensive recliner, liked to watch TV most of the day. He took frequent naps and had cocktails with Liz and Kate as he cooked super nightly. He liked old movies, the *History Channel*, and the area professional sports teams.

Liz still controlled the money and took daily walks with several retired women instructors and union government workers. They discussed women's issues, the need for Planned Parenthood, the deplorable conditions of the homeless, the need for better school lunch programs, how terrible guns were, and how they had succeeded by diligence and good decisions while their husbands simply rode along in a privileged system. At least twice a week, Liz and Kate met with the university widows' group, drank wine, and planned theater outings or travel arrangements. Liz was pleased with her past, her childhood background, and her university education which taught her to be open-minded, never judgmental, and to forgive all. Liz adamantly proclaimed herself a conservative while insisting she always voted for the person and not an ideology. Liz had not voted for a conservative in over forty years.

From high atop the hill overlooking Astoria, the river, and the school district, with their government pensions and wine, they postulated, pontificated, and opinioned in concert. Liz, confident, pleased, and contented, validated her fair and open-minded view of everything with her associates. At times she fretted and stewed with Kate over the closed-minded parents who attended the community meetings and complained about sex education, shared bathroom facilities, normalizing transgenderism, or teaching evolution in the district.

Liz's bubble had taken on various shapes, but she felt it was rounding nicely for this time in her life. Liz got special attention and sympathy among here friends and family because of her sincere political views, volunteering, and her daughter's suicide. In a discussion one evening, Liz asked Kate how she felt about church.

Kate said, "Oh my, I have not been to church in years. Mother still goes quite often though."

Liz replied, "Yes, I know. I heard they have a new lady priest at Astoria Christian. I thought we might check her out sometime."

Kate responded, "Yes, our church has kept up with the times. They not only allowed women priests, but this diocese now has a female bishop."

As Liz prepared to leave, they decided to attend a new Saturday night service at Astoria Christian the following evening. Liz said to Kate, "I will pick you up at eight sharp! Be ready."

Returning home after the church service, Liz pulled her Mercedes into the garage. She noticed the access door for the cat had not been closed. At night, Kenny usually called the cat inside and closed the door. She stepped outside and called for the cat. It did not come. She left the cat door open and proceeded into the house, thinking the cat might be with Kenny. Placing her coat across a chair, she headed to the TV room to see if Kenny was awake or if he had gone to bed. As she entered the room, she noticed the big screen TV was on but not very loud. On TV, a blonde was actively participating in a sex act Liz had never envisioned. As the blonde gyrated and sighed, Liz turned toward Kenny. Kenny was motionless staring straightforward at the screen. He did not move or blink.

Astoria Church

Liz said, "Good gosh, Kenny! Did the cat step on the remote and change the channel?"

Kenny did not respond.

Liz reached for the remote control in Kenny's hand. His hand was cold and did not move. Prying the controller from Kenny's hand, Liz turned toward the big screen. A second male entered the room on screen. Watching intently, Liz's eyes never left the screen, or the naked bodies, or the male anatomies as they assumed positions. Sitting on the arm of Kenny's recliner, she settled in making herself comfortable. Making no attempt to change channels, Liz was focused. Her bubble was expanding to include pornography.

"Do not be deceived: Bad company ruins good morals." (1 Corinthians 15:33)

"Husband, live with your wife in an understanding way, showing honor, since they are heirs with you of the grace of life." (1 Peter 3:7)

Jerry Hanson. 2018

PAWN TO BISHOP III

Samuel Thorsten's grandfather, Johan, came to Kansas to serve a seven-year indentureship to his brother-in-law, Hendrick Schmidt. Johan was in trouble with the law in Norway, and his oldest sister, Ingrid, through Johan's mother, arranged passage for Johan from Northern Norway through Russia to the United States. Johan was nineteen years old. Exactly four years ago to the day, Johan was trapping polar bears for European zoos with his father. They were on the ice fields far north of the Arctic Circle. Checking the trap lines, Johan's father gasped, grasped his chest for breath, and sunk to his knees. He was suffering a heart attack. Johan's father died in his arms on the frozen Arctic Ocean. Upset and distraught over his inability to save his father, Johan had to transport his father's body home to his family. Attending the funeral at the local Lutheran Church with his five sisters and mother, Johan was sick with worry over how to provide for his family.

Trying to help make ends meet, Johan joined a group of young men from the Lutheran Church and started a fishing venture. Nine young men in three dory boats set out each morning in the darkness to head far out into the rough and cold Atlantic to fish. They were good at their dangerous task of deep cold water fishing and brought home plentiful catches. They shared equally in the profits of the catch after supplies and boat charges were paid. The only market for their catch was the local cannery. The British government owned the cannery. In accordance with British dictates, the cannery began

Dory Boat

to purchase British vessel catches before accepting local fishermen catches. In February, the cannery began a practice of buying a limited amount of fish. When that limit was filled, no more purchases were made. Many a day, local Norwegian fishermen couldn't sell their catches. There was simply too much fish for family consumption, so the catches rotted and became garden fertilizer.

This was the beginning of Johan's troubles. Five of the nine fishing partners successfully pulled off a scheme to damage the tall brick smoke stack of the British cannery in defiance of the fish buying policy. Within a few days, everyone in the village knew the names of the smoke stack vandals. Pastor Borg came to the Thorsten house. He told Mrs. Thorsten, "Johan is angry, misguided, sinful, and very unruly. The pastor added, "Johan must get out of Norway before he is arrested and sent to prison!" That is how nineteen-year-old Johan Thorsten ended up as a farm hand on Hendrick and Ingrid Schmidt's Kansas wheat farm.

Johan hated dryland farming, flat barren plains, no mountains and no bodies of water for miles around. Johan longed for the mountains and fjords of Norway. Working hard long hours kept his mind on the tasks at hand and time passed. When the seven-year indentureship ended, Johan not knowing what laid in his future left Kansas. Missing Norway, he wondered aimlessly and drifted north toward Minnesota. Speaking poor English, he managed to pick up odd farm jobs. Along the way, he met Mae Brown. She worked as a cook's helper on the Crooked-S ranch near Saint Cloud. After knowing one another for less than a month, Mae and Johan eloped with all their belongings and headed back to Kansas. Hendrick Schmidt helped register them for a government land grant near the Schmidt farm. There were several other Norwegian families who did dryland farming thereby. Johan and Mae had six children and tripled the size of their land grant farm. Johan worked as much as eighteen ours per day, seven days each week. Mae raised the family and they all helped Johan however and whenever they could. Johan did not trust the government, but Mae encouraged him to borrow from the local farm bank. Johan was ambitious and borrowed money to buy hogs, raise and fatten them on his wheat, and sell them to the Kansas City hog market.

Johan's Hogs

The dust bowl hit mid-America and the great depression hit everyone. The Thorstens, like everyone, suffered. For six years, the prairie winds blew and blew. Johan's seed was ripped from the soil as fast as he could plant. He borrowed more money for seed only to have it blown away. With a limited wheat crop, Johan had to cut the size of his hog holdings. He was losing money. The government confiscated his wheat. It was needed for flour mills to make bread in large cities. City people were starving. The government gave Johan one dollar for each of his hogs, shot them, and buried them in a ditch. Johan decided to horde the money received from the government. He did not pay his creditors or the bank. Taxes were due on the farm, which Johan did not pay. Johan had no more credit for buying planting seed or brood sows. Johan and Mae prayed for guidance. The Lutheran pastor came by the farm but spent most of his time asking for donations from Johan's government money. He spoke in Biblical terms about the need for sharing at this time. He expressed no concern for Johan and Mae's circumstance or plight. This was the same pastor that kicked Leonard, their oldest son, out of Sunday school stating, "He has a devious soul." That night Johan and Mae held hands, discussed their options, and asked for guidance from above. With six kids and everything they owned piled onto an overloaded buckboard, they headed north in the dark of night. America was no longer the land of dreams for the Thorstens.

Nearly out of food and provisions, weary, tired, and nearing the Canadian border, the Thorstens stopped and set up camp. They were on the banks of a very large, wind-blown, and rough lake. The lake was surrounded by snow-capped mountains, covered with thick lush forests. Lake Powell reminded Johan of the Norwegian fjords.

Early in the morning, Johan cobbled together a crude log raft and went fishing. He caught several large trout and several salmon. By the camp fire that morning the family ate better than they had in months. Johan and Mae settled on Lake Powell, raised their family, and were good neighbors. They were always suspicious and fearful of the government and banks and uncertain about pastors.

Mae tried to bring some aspect of church and religion into the family. They occasionally attended the Lutheran Church which

Mother's Quilts

reminded Johan once again of Norway. They went a few times for the kid's sake, but it never worked out as a permanent thing to do.

Mae Thorsten held the deepest love and affection for her two daughters. She had concluded her rough and tumble boys could hold their own in the great outdoors. She fretted to herself about what the future held for her daughters. When Samuel's mother, who grew up without parents, married Leonard, she wanted desperately to become one of Mae's daughters. That never happened. There was no room in Mae's heart for an outside British woman. Observing the occasional visits to the local Lutheran Church, Samuel's mother assumed the way into the Thorsten family was to become a good God-fearing Lutheran. She did. In fact, she became more Lutheran than Martin Luther.

Mother was on committees, tithed regularly, taught Sunday school, volunteered for all sorts of duty, and quilted many a blanket to give to the various Indian tribes. Mother was known wide and far in the Lutheran Church and Ladies Circles. The main Lutheran Church in Powell County was so successful, it sponsored and shepherded into being seven satellite Lutheran Churches. Mother was part of that effort and remained a stalwart member at the main church. The main church had two full-time pastors, two associate pastors, and a full administrative staff and was broadcast live on the local radio station every Sunday morning. Mother had many church friends, and her best friend, Regina Boldbag, was the head musician. Mother escorted her six boys to church on Sunday mornings whether they wanted to attend or not, that is, until they graduated grade school. Then, church attendance ended. Samuel, her middle son, was one of the non-attendees.

Like Leonard, Samuel felt closeness to God did not have much bearing on attending church. Leonard, Samuel, and his brothers attended church on major religious holidays for Mother's sake. When Samuel married, his wife agreed to be married in the main Powell Lutheran Church which pleased his mother greatly. Samuel moved from Powell for over twenty years and then returned. Their pre-teen son and daughter were promptly invited to attend the Lutheran Church by their grandmother. Samuel encouraged them to attend, and Grandmother showed them off like prize horses at the county fair. To show support for their children attending church and because

Pastor Bjorn Eliasson

it pleased Mother, Samuel and his wife began attending church. Soon Samuel's wife was teaching Sunday school, and Samuel was solicited to be on the church council. Later that year, Samuel was chosen to be on the board of elders and asked to be president of the congregation. Samuel felt he was never worthy enough to be on any council let alone a board of elders. Samuel shared Leonard's Norwegian last name and his mother's good name. Samuel was elected by proclamation. Mother was proud and pleased. The local Norwegian farmers and fishermen were happy to have a Norwegian, at least in name, in a church leadership role.

Coming from a business environment, Samuel soon realized the church was in financial trouble. The younger families were attending the satellite churches as the old folks stayed at the main church. The older members were very generous with their tithes, but when one of them passed on, the weekly income dropped considerably. Samuel learned that a large portion of their estates in many cases was gifted to the Lutheran Diocese. Most of their estates were valued in the hundreds of thousands of dollars. The local membership was shrinking and reserves were being depleted to pay monthly expenses. The congregation was slowly and steadily losing membership and revenue, while the diocese was growing wealthy. When Samuel and the finance committee addressed these issues with Head Pastor Bjorn Eliasson, he acted disinterested, appeared unconcerned, and was disengaged. Eliasson had been at the church for seventeen years. The old Norwegian families held him in high regard. He was a personal friend of Bishop Issac Alford, held PhDs in Greek and Hebrew studies, and could quote Bible versus verbatim. When it was suggested for financial reasons to downsize and have young Associate Pastor Avril assigned elsewhere, Eliasson exploded. He defiantly stood up and loudly rebuked and admonished the council and finance committee. Shaking his finger at the committee members, he sternly stated, "Focus on membership, fellowship, and fund-raising! Stay out of the management of staff. That is my job!"

The following week at the Wednesday Bible study, Eliasson was curt and caustic to Samuel and his wife. When Samuel's wife asked Eliasson an honest question in search of understanding, Eliasson sharply replied, "No one can reach heaven without believing in Jesus Christ. That is absolutely and irrefutably the truth!"

Dissatisfied and taken back, she continued her questioning, "What about all the other people in the world? Are all the people in China, who may have not heard of Jesus, doomed to hell?"

Eliasson retorted, "They are doomed to hell! Don't you read the scriptures?"

On the way home, Samuel's wife stated, "I can't accept that God would banish to hell people of the world who are in the dark about Jesus." Furthermore, she added, "I do not care for the way Pastor Eliasson treated me, his arrogant attitude, nor his approach to pastoring and teaching! I am ready for a different church."

Samuel was also becoming less and less enthusiastic about going to church and especially going to the church committee meetings. Mother was gleefully attending quilting circle, choir practice, and Bible study. Samuel's wife was preparing to quietly exit her Sunday school roll. Elma Olson, the church secretary, noticed Samuel's change in church interest, lack of enthusiasm, and noticeably not coming around the parish. She asked him to go to lunch. At lunch Elma quickly blurted out, "Myself and others cannot help but notice you are not satisfied with our church. You are not coming around like you used to. We desperately need your leadership. Things are out of control financially. The membership is dwindling. The staff is unmotivated and not working very hard. There are other troubling and unacceptable things going on in our church!" She repeated, "We need you here, Samuel!"

Samuel responded, "Elma, I do not know what you mean by 'other troubling and unacceptable things going on in our church'. I will not get into innuendo or gossip. Gossiping ruins fellowship and the worshiping experience in a congregation."

Elma responded, "Some stalwart and long-time members of the congregation took three days off to drive to church headquarters and speak to Bishop Alford. They asked to privately address some church concerns with the bishop."

Samuel said, "Elma, are you telling me you knew of their trip and purpose, yet the council is in the dark? I as president did not know about this."

Elma responded, "They knew their visit and purpose might cause a lot of trouble. They wanted to keep it quiet. They feel Bishop Alford will do the right thing."

Samuel had not touched his salad and said, "Elma, this has been a very troubling lunch. I am not disturbed with you, but I am disturbed that congregational members go around their elected council and president. Furthermore, you have not told me what the other trouble is. Can you not tell me?"

Elma said, "I have been here for over thirty years, and I know all of our members like brothers and sisters. I promised to keep this issue a secret. I cannot tell you at this time. But I will tell them of your concern about being left out of the loop with the bishop."

Samuel replied, "Elma, I can tell them myself! Surely you understand myself and the council need to know what is going on in our congregation! We are the elected leaders and a vigilante posse should not be going off to represent the church to the bishop."

Elma said, "You know I count the tithes and these are our very largest givers! They mean well."

A couple weeks passed and Samuel dropped by the church office to pick up his mail. A stranger gleefully greeted him near the mail boxes. He held out his hand and said, "You must be the man I am looking for. I'm Pastor Mike Clark. Bishop Alford sent me over to spend a couple months helping with the clergy's workload."

Samuel stepped back and slowly said, "Oh, I did not know you were coming."

Clark responded, "The timing was a little hurried, but it has been in the works for a few months."

Samuel said, "Welcome aboard. Did the bishop send along some funds for your salary?"

Clark chuckled and said, "The diocese pays my salary, but the local church will be on the hook for my expenses. I keep those pretty low however."

Samuel said, "Welcome again. I'm sure I will see you around."

Pastor Clark made special efforts to seek Samuel out and spent a great deal of time with him, far more time than any of the other pastors. It came out he knew a great deal about Samuel, his family,

Pastor Mike Clark

and especially his mother. Clark said, "I understand you were quite the baseball player in Powell, but you went off to school to become a dentist." He continued, "I was a good baseball player and made it to the Augusta Bee's, a triple A club."

Samuel's interest peaked and he responded, "Really, what position did you play?"

He said, "Pitcher. I was not a power pitcher. I had a curve ball nobody could hit."

Samuel said, "Yeah, I had a little trouble with those wicked curve balls myself." Then Samuel said, "Pastor Clark?"

But he was interrupted as Clark said, "Please call me Mike."

Samuel continued, "Okay, Mike, my question is why are you here and why did I not know about your coming?"

Mike said, "Well I've been meaning to talk to you about that and I wanted to do that today. Do you have some time?"

"I've got all afternoon!" replied Samuel.

Pastor Clark said, "Can we go to the library and talk?"

They started toward the library and Clark began speaking, "Bishop Alford called me out of sabbatical last month to report here in Powell. I flew to the bishop's office for a briefing and the next day flew out here. The diocese is well aware of the shrinking membership and financial pressure on this church. Older members are dying, and although they leave large estates to the diocese, them and their tithing are absent from this church. We are called to increase the membership in this church and get it financially healthy once again. It has also been reported that other members of the congregation are migrating to other churches, and yet others have reduced their tithing. The Anders, Danson, Bork, Hageman, and Lawson families have always kept the bishop informed about the comings and goings in this congregation. You know the bishop is the nephew of both the Borks and Anders. But to cut to the chase, there are serious problems within the Pastor Eliasson family. If you had not noticed the large four-bedroom parsonage is only being lived in by Pastor Eliasson. His wife and her church car have been gone for nearly four months. Two of their children attend Lutheran College on full-ride church scholarships paid by this church. The congregation has been told one of the children

The Powell Church

has mononucleosis, and Mrs. Eliasson is nursing them so they can remain in college. The truth is Mrs. Eliasson caught Pastor Eliasson in a very compromising position with Associate Pastor Miss Avril. The Eliassons prayed together and he begged for her forgiveness. She forgave him. But two weeks later she caught them together in the oldest boy's parsonage bedroom. He swore to the bishop they only needed a private place to talk, but apparently Mrs. Eliasson did not buy the explanation. She told her church friends she had to be with her daughter at college. She left and has not returned."

Pastor Clark continued, "Eliasson told the bishop there were some issues in their marriage but did not elaborate. If you did not know, Bishop Alford and Pastor Eliasson graduated seminary together. They are long-time friends. A few weeks passed and at a retreat, Eliasson confessed to the bishop of marital problems over the past couple years. Eliasson reported his wife was not interested in the Bible, the church, or being a pastor's wife. He added this past year her attitude had worsened. He admitted to the bishop she had been absent from the marital bed and recently vacated the parsonage to help his daughter. Eliasson was confident she would return after some rest and they would patch things up. Eliasson assured the bishop things would return to normal. He never brought up Miss Avril."

Mike said, "Bishop Alford accepted the explanation and agreed with Eliasson's assessment. They prayed together in hopes this issue would blow over. However, about a month ago some of your parishioners came to visit the bishop and reported things were getting worse. For example, Elma reported she had seen Eliasson snuggling, fondling, and kissing Miss Avril in the choir room. Thereafter, she could not help but notice an overly cozy relationship between the two of them. She had observed this behavior several times but did not know what to do. Then gossip began to spread in the congregation after some teenage boys, out pulling pranks one evening, spied Eliasson and Avril together in the parsonage bathtub. They told their parents. Secretly the gossip is spreading family to family throughout the congregation. I have been sent here to pastor to Pastor Eliasson. I need to help him repent and find his way. The bishop's orders are to rehabilitate Eliasson back into his leadership role as head pastor of this church. I will need your help in that effort. We must hold the congregation together and your mother is a large part of that effort."

Samuel said, "Do you mean to tell me my mother is aware of all this mess?"

Mike said, "No, your mother is a naive pure heart and kind soul. She and her friends are such an integral part of this congregation that they will have a tremendous calming effect as this gets out. You are in a key leadership role and have the Thorsten name. That stands tall with these Norwegians and the congregation."

Samuel responded, "Well this is a fine mess, Mike. What is your plan to move forward?"

Mike said, "Most of the folks here do not know about these circumstances, but it is slowly and steadily leaking out. I don't think Elma can sit on it much longer herself. Some of the folks will overlook the transgressions, but others are puritanical and will quit tithing or go elsewhere. My job is to pastor and help Eliasson repent and get well. The bishop wants him to stay here. I suggest you let the pastors handle the worship and religion aspects, but you will have to manage the business and social and financial side of the church. What do you say?"

Samuel replied, "This is not at all what I come to church for! How do you feel about Eliasson?"

Mike replied, "He is a bit pompous, a little arrogant about his lofty education, he thinks he should be bishop, and he looks down upon my lesser education, credentials, and mediocre baseball background. But I am not here to judge but to do God's work in healing a fallen brother."

Samuel said, "Well that sure is an easy mouthful to say when the finances, membership, and enthusiasm are crumbling around us."

Mike said, "Well that is where we are today. It is not that dire. Surely you know the diocese could always use their funds to shore up the church financially, but they want the congregation to pay their own way."

After being quiet, Mike offered a prayer. They shook hands and parted to go their separate ways.

Over the next few weeks, Samuel continued attending church and going to meetings as if things were fine. His mother was kept in the dark, but she was noticing cracks in the church attendance and fellowship. The council tried to increase Sunday school participation for kids and teenagers, and more families were attending, but giving was inadequate to cover the expenses. One day Myrna Flanders, from the church council, asked Samuel to lunch. She told him of the growing rumors of Pastor Eliasson and Pastor Avril's affair. She also said, "Even some of the families who were close to Mrs. Eliasson have contacted her about why she has not returned to Powell. She has told them the truth."

She also stated, "Many of us are not giving regularly because we are so disturbed with this situation in our church. I am going to bring this situation and issue up at the next council meeting and wanted you to know. Pastor Eliasson will be there and it might get ugly."

Samuel replied, "Thank you, Myrna, for giving me a heads up. Do what you must do."

Samuel returned to the church and sought out Pastor Clark and advised him of the lunch conversation with Myrna. Samuel asked him for his input.

Clark said, "He would advise Eliasson about the subject being addressed at the council meeting, so he was not blindsided." He cautioned Samuel, "The congregation must deal with this matter in a Christian manner!"

At the next council meeting, Myrna brought up the Eliasson and Avril transgressions. The only pastor to attend was Clark, and he offered the excuse that Eliasson and the others were busy.

Myrna stated, "She would no longer serve on the council and would attend church elsewhere if this matter was not dealt with and put to bed."

Myrna with others chiming in said, "The membership is half what it was last year, the finances are unacceptable, we are running out of reserve funds, and the congregational warmth and fellowship have become cold and distant."

Others rang their hands and said, "We must not judge but go slowly to let Clark help heal Eliasson."

Church Services

Then Aaron Anders said, "His wife had talked to Mrs. Eliasson this past week and she is filing for divorce."

Pastor Clark said, "I have not heard that. Can you verify that, Aaron?"

Borge Swenson, Mrs. Eliasson's lifelong friend, interjected, "Yes, it is true. Trudy is filing for divorce. She has an attorney, all the paperwork is in order, and she will file this week. I am going to be with her for support."

The meeting got quiet and Samuel asked for the council's direction regarding the matter.

Pastor Clark said, "Let's wait a couple weeks."

Samuel tersely retorted, "This game of untruths, dishonesty, and looking the other way has been going on for months! Enough is enough! The congregation suffers, fellowship is stunted, the joy of worship succumbs to evil! I'm done with this charade! This is not just about Eliasson! What about Miss Avril? What about Elma? What about Mrs. Eliasson, and most of all what are the youth of this congregation to learn? We keep a head pastor in place after his improper behavior as a pastor, his improprieties on church grounds and church facilities, his leading a young vulnerable female pastor astray, and dishonoring his marriage vows. All of this because he has a PhD and is a buddy with the bishop! In my opinion, this must be dealt with swiftly!"

Samuel had said far more than he intended. The silence was deafening in the meeting room. Then Regina Boldbag said, "If such a learned man as Pastor Eliasson is defamed or let go, I will quit this church!" Regina then noisily stood, with great commotion grabbed her belongings, and defiantly marched out of the meeting.

After midnight, the council voted to hold a congregational meeting the coming Saturday and requested Pastor Clark address the full congregation.

Saturday came and a large part of the congregation attended the meeting. Once the home-made sandwiches, salads, and coffees provided by the auxiliary ladies were consumed, contrary to plans Pastor Eliasson stood up, commanded the room's attention, and said, "I am not sure why we are congregating here today, but thanked everyone for coming and suggested they all go home and enjoy the rest of the weekend."

He began to offer a dismissal prayer when Pastor Clark interrupted and said, "There are some issues the council wants to discuss with the congregation." He continued, "Where is our esteemed president?"

Samuel was caught completely off guard with this turn of events. He slowly rose, and with a heavy heart, whispered under his breath, "Lord, help me!" as he walked to the front of the room. Eliasson watched him intently as he slowly came forward. Samuel began to speak and said, "I know, and most of you know, there have been some ugly rumors circulating through the congregation. I do not know if there is truth in the rumors, but I do know as Christians we should not be judging or spreading rumors. Our congregation is shrinking in membership, and we have serious financial concerns. Knowing this, I would like to ask all of you to search your hearts for what is right for you and what is right for our church and pray for congregational guidance. Now, I think we all should go home and enjoy our weekend as Pastor Eliasson has suggested."

Samuel asked Pastor Clark to lead a closing prayer. The congregation disbanded, but numerous groups huddled together, quietly and secretly talked in the parking lot.

On Sunday morning, Pastor Eliasson and Pastor Avril were not available for the services. Elma advised that they had gone to Regina Boldbag for a morning brunch. Regina also was absent and an organist was not available for the broadcast service. Samuel learned later his mother had been invited to the Boldbag's brunch but chose to attend church. Pastor Clark was left to conduct the services, and what was left of the choir provided music. The radio broadcast was lacking.

After much thought and prayer, Samuel called for an emergency joint meeting of the elders and council. From the clergy, only Pastor Clark was invited. On a vote that passed by a simple majority, the council decided to request the bishop to reassign both Eliasson and Avril and to assign Pastor Clark as interim head pastor. Pastor Clark was in agreement. Samuel was charged with calling the bishop the next day and advise him of the council's request.

At 10:00 a.m. on Wednesday, Samuel called Bishop Alford to relay the council's wishes. The bishop was unfriendly, cold, and uncommunicative. Finally, the bishop said, "I have heard about all this." Then he said, "I am coming to your church this Friday to help heal the congregation."

Samuel replied, "Great, can I make some arrangements and accommodations for you?"

The bishop curtly replied, "No, I will stay in the parsonage with Bjorn. We were college roommates if you didn't know."

Samuel replied, "Okay, then we will see you Friday. Travel safely."

Samuel was troubled and concerned. He felt alone and wished he had never gotten involved in his mother's church. He knew something was askew with the bishop. Samuel sought out Pastor Clark and told him his concerns.

Mike told him, "I cannot get involved. I work for the bishop and my job is to pastor to fallen pastors."

Samuel asked, "Do you think the bishop will reassign Eliasson and Avril?"

Clark replied, "Probably not. He might reassign Avril but not Eliasson. You will most likely have to refuse to pay them and demand they exit the parsonage and church premises because the bishop will side with Eliasson over the council, elders, and congregation. In fact, the bishop will most likely scold the congregation and especially you folks in leadership."

He continued, "The bishop's position is that transgressions and sin occur. The world and our lives are filled with sin. From his experiences and belief, he feels this will all blow over. He wants the congregation to act like true Christians and forgive Eliasson and Avril."

Samuel was now truly troubled. He called a special urgent council meeting and relayed his concerns. Pastor Clark, to his credit, relayed to the council exactly what he had told Samuel about the bishop's views. After lengthy discussion and debate, the council voted that Eliasson and Avril needed to leave the parish. Conditions were set:

1) If the bishop transfers Eliasson, transfers Avril, and appoints Pastor Clark as interim pastor.

Bishop Issac Alford

2) Then the council would forgive the $25,000 cash loan to
    Eliasson, pay Eliasson and Avril each three months separa-
    tion salary, and honor the church paid scholarships for the
    Eliasson children's college tuition.

The treasurer was to provide Samuel with signed checks, a
credit forgiveness letter, and Samuel was to meet with Eliasson and
the bishop when the bishop came to town. There would be no meeting with the elders and council with the bishop or Eliasson or Avril.
Eliasson was to vacate the parsonage and premises as soon as possible
but no later than the end of the month. All church property and
church cars were to be returned to Elma. Regina Boldbag and two
others swiftly walked out of the meeting. Samuel asked for a vote and
for the secretary to record the actions and results for the record. The
remaining members voted unanimously in approval.

Friday at noon, the bishop arrived and was met by Eliasson.
Elma called Samuel and said Eliasson and the bishop wanted to meet
with the council. Samuel advised Elma he had arranged to meet with
Eliasson and the bishop at 4:00 p.m. at the parsonage.

Samuel told Elma, "That is where and when we will meet, as
previously discussed and planned!"

Samuel asked Elma to advise them accordingly and confirm the
parsonage meeting.

Elma then said, "Pastor Eliasson had told her to arrange for a
council meeting at 7:30 p.m."

Samuel responded, "Tell him okay, but do not arrange a meeting
until you hear back from me after my 4:00 p.m. meeting with them."

Elma said, "Well okay, Samuel, but this could get me in trouble
or fired from my job."

Samuel responded, "Elma, I assure you, you will not be in trouble or fired from your job."

At 3:58 p.m., Samuel knocked on the parsonage door. There
was no answer. He waited and knocked again. There was still no
answer. He waited until 4:15 p.m. and called Elma.

Samuel said, "Elma, I am at the parsonage for my meeting with the
bishop and Pastor Eliasson. They are not here and it is now 4:15 p.m."

JERRY HANSON

The Kitchen Table

Elma replied, "They walked downtown about a half hour ago to have some coffee and chat. Do you want me to call them?"

Samuel said, "Elma, would please? Call me back with their response."

Ten minutes passed and Elma called Samuel, "They are walking back and will arrive shortly. They want to meet in the pastor's office."

Samuel held his tongue and said, "Elma, please recall them and tell them I am waiting at the parsonage per our planned arrangements! I will be waiting for them here! Elma, I am sorry if I appear short. I am a little frustrated with them but not at you."

Another thirty minutes passed, and the bishop and Pastor Eliasson casually sauntered up to parsonage steps sipping lattes. They were distant and unfriendly. Eliasson proceeded to open the door to the parsonage.

Samuel said, "We have some matters to discuss. May I come in?"

There was no answer, but they all entered the parsonage and took seats at the kitchen table.

The bishop said, "So what's on your mind?"

Samuel said, "The first order of business is I want you to know I represent the elders and the council, and I am relaying their directives to you."

The bishop responded, "My, that sounds very serious!"

Samuel replied, "It is not only serious. It is troubling!"

The bishop tersely said, "Okay, well let's get to it then. We have a council meeting at seven thirty."

Samuel said, "Before there will be a council meeting, the matters of this meeting must be resolved."

Once again, the bishop sharply said, "Well get on with it then!"

Samuel began, "Bishop, on behalf of the council, I am requesting you to immediately reassign Pastor Eliasson and Associate Pastor Avril to somewhere else and appoint Pastor Clark as our interim pastor until a replacement is found." Samuel turned to Pastor Eliasson and said, "I am sorry, but this is the council's wishes and they feel it is for the good of the congregation and yourself."

Eliasson responded, "Well the council is only an elected body. The congregation is the authoritative body!"

Samuel responded, "Are you disputing the council's decision, because surely you know they have the appointed authority?"

The bishop interceded and said, "Well there are two issues here. First, I as bishop have the authority to assign pastors or not assign pastors, and secondly the congregation at large has the authority to accept a pastor or dismiss them."

Samuel said, "I understand what both of you are saying and do not wish to be argumentative or disrespectful. I am only doing the wishes of the council, and once again I am asking you Bishop Alford to make the assignments and reassignment effective immediately. Will you honor those requests?"

The bishop responded, "I know you are in a difficult position, but in church life, these issues arise more often than you might think. Evil raises its ugly head for a while and then congregations calms down and the issues go away. You and the council with all your good intentions are overreacting and I cannot in good conscience reassign Pastor Eliasson. I will consider reassigning Pastor Avril and Pastor Clark can stay here as long as necessary to do his assigned job of helping Pastor Eliasson. After three months, the local church will have to pay Pastor Clark's salary. I guess we are through here!" and he began to rise.

Samuel sternly said, "No, bishop! We are not through here!" The bishop settled back into his chair surprised at Samuel's sharp rebuttal. He exchanged quizzical glances with Eliasson.

Samuel continued, "The council has the complete financial authority over spending and local church assets. I am hereby advising you and Pastor Eliasson that effective immediately no further payments of any sort will be made to Pastor Eliasson or Pastor Avril. The parsonage is to be vacated immediately by Pastor Eliasson, and I want the keys for his church car. Additionally, if we cannot resolve these matters here and now, monthly scholarship payments for the Eliasson children's tuition will cease, and the $25,000 loan is immediately due. I am sorry to be so bold, but you have given me no choice."

Eliasson and Alford stared in disbelief at Samuel. They sat looking perplexed and dumbfounded. Finally the bishop said, "Is that final?"

Samuel said, "What is final is Pastor Eliasson and Pastor Avril must leave as soon as possible. That is the council's final decision.

If you will do the assignments as requested, and Eliasson and Avril leave immediately, then the council will forgive the $25,000 loan and honor the scholarship payments. I have checks here for three months of separation pay for Eliasson and Avril. That is not only the final offer. It is the only offer."

Eliasson eyes teared up and he said, "I know I have made some mistakes, but I never thought it would come to this."

Samuel said, "I am sorry, Pastor Eliasson, but this is of your doings. This is for the best. The council wishes you well and prays you get well." Eliasson arose and slowly ambled out of the kitchen toward the living room.

Bishop Alford sat stone-faced, tapping his fingers on the table. He curtly said, "It looks like you thought this through, Samuel."

Samuel replied, "How do you mean I thought this through? It's the council's wishes, and it is what needs to be done. This congregation is falling apart."

The bishop wryly smiled and retorted, "Regardless of what you think should be done, it may still all fall apart because of your actions. This is not all on the back of Pastor Eliasson due to his missteps."

Samuel said, "I am not prepared to debate that or any other issue with you, bishop. I need an answer on the business at hand."

The bishop said, "I'll go talk with Bjorn."

Samuel waited for over thirty minutes before Alford and Eliasson returned to the kitchen.

The bishop said, "We have prayed about it and we accept your offer."

Samuel said, "There will be no council meeting tonight," as he handed Eliasson his check and the letter of debt forgiveness. Samuel shook Eliasson's hand and wished him well. Eliasson disappeared from the kitchen.

He asked Bishop Alford to give Pastor Avril her check when he spoke with her. He thanked the bishop for his agreement and for coming to the church during this difficult time. The bishop took the check and sternly glared at Samuel. Samuel awkwardly paused and began to offer a handshake only to observe the bishop was withdrawing. They did not shake hands or exchange salutations. Samuel gathered his things and left.

That night Samuel telephoned Aaron Anders and advised he was stepping down from the presidency and council. As vice president, Aaron would become president. Aaron probed Samuel about how things had gone with Pastor Eliasson and the bishop. Samuel responded, "The reassignments would be immediate and the financial agreements the council had wanted were to be put in place."

Aaron continued to query Samuel about the meeting, the circumstances, and individual reactions. Samuel was tired and did not want to talk. He told Aaron, "I am drained of energy and need to go. They said goodbye."

Pastor Clark held the service for Sunday by himself, and neither Samuel nor his family attended service. Samuel's mother went to church and then dropped by his home. She said, "The service was very somber. Regina has gone to another church and the rumor is you and the council strong-armed the bishop and ran Eliasson and Avril out of town. People are upset."

Samuel responded, "Mother, I am so sorry to have gotten into the middle of your church. I thought you would be pleased. There is much more to this story, but I do not want to spread gossip and hurt the church or individuals further. It will come out over time, but I hope you continue to worship and do your good works."

Samuel's mother said, "Well, there sure are a lot of unhappy folks. Oh, would you and your family like to go to dinner with your father and me tonight at Rudy's Diner?"

Samuel said, "Of course, Mother."

Halfway through dinner at Rudy's, Samuel looked up to see Bishop Alford and Pastor Jeremy Alford, the bishop's brother from Lutheran Services, coming toward them on their way to a table. Mother spotted them and gleefully and merrily said, "Hello."

They both gushed over Mother ignoring Samuel, his wife, their children, and his father. Upon departing from their table, Mother said, "They are the most wonderful people I have ever met. Don't you agree?"

Samuel responded, "Yes, Mother, I'm sure God has a special place for them!"

Except for Samuel's mother, not one single person from the congregation, church staff, or clergy had any contact or a conversation with Samuel since that evening in the parsonage and after his conversation with Arron Anders. Even Samuel's newest best friend, Pastor Clark had disappeared from Samuel's life.

It is early Saturday morning, and Samuel and his son David are traveling to an out-of-town soccer game. It was nearing 6:00 a.m. and Samuel and David had been driving for over an hour. They exited the rural highway, at a rundown service station to get gas. There was a twenty-four-hour convenience store inside. Walking to the store, Samuel passed a body lying beside the garbage dumpster. It was a male. He was curled up in a fetal position, grasping a brown bag with a container spilling alcohol onto the frozen asphalt. Several empty beer bottles were strewn nearby. He had passed out, and his body shuddered every so often in the cold. His mangled and matted hair lay in vomit on a soiled handmade quilt beneath his head. Samuel recognized the quilt, the material, and the pattern.

With his mind still on the man and the quilt, Samuel and David entered the convenience store. They paid for the gas and purchased some doughnuts, coffee, and a soft drink. As Samuel departed the store he thought *'mother does not choose who, how, or where her handmade quilts get utilized. He thought about the Lutheran Church. He knew churches and religious organizations were composed of human beings, people with flaws. Unfortunately, the printed Word could not be brought forward into the world and be distributed without organizations. For all its weaknesses, shortcomings, and injustices, the church was necessary, not only for the perpetuation of the faith but to serve as a place for those who are searching for the truth.*

Entering the highway, Samuel suddenly stopped the car. He popped the trunk open and exited the car. From the trunk he removed a handmade quilt his mother insisted he carry in case of cold weather or an emergency. Leaving his door wide open and trunk up, Samuel walked over to the dumpster and placed the quilt over the man on the ground. As Samuel reentered the car he said to David, "I suppose Grandmother's quilt might give some comfort to that fellow?"

Service Station

Munching on his doughnut, David looked toward the dumpster and then back at Samuel. David paused for a moment and then said, "Dad, that was very kind of you."

As David finished his doughnut and they drove off, he said, "I think we can score from midfield on this team if we attack in transition."

Samuel and his wife retired. His mother and father are deceased. His children are in college. Pastor and Mrs. Eliasson are divorced. He lives with Miss Avril and they were assigned to serve a very small rural church. Their church struggles with finances and membership. Pastor Eliasson writes contributing articles to the national church's monthly publications. Eliasson and Miss Avril have never married.

Pastor Clark continues to "pastors to pastors." After years of service, he was seated as a member of the national church clergy council and determines promotions. Bishop Bjorn Alford became head of the national church. Pastor Paul Alford received one more vote than Pastor Eliasson and was appointed bishop.

The Powell Church returned to financial stability. Regina Boldbag retired as head musician and organ player. Elma Olson is office manager and supervises the administrative staff.

David's team won the soccer game and he scored two goals from midfield.

Samuel is concerned his children's college curricula are biased against religion and God. He worries their worship experiences negatively affect their outlook on church. He accepts organization and hierarchy, but chess matches with the clergy are not pleasant worship experiences.

"God is at work within you…helping you do what he wants." (Philippians 2:13)

"The Lord will lead you…he will not fail you or abandon you, do not loose courage or be afraid." (Deuteronomy 31:8)

Jerry Hanson. 2019

JACOB'S BUSINESS

Grandpa Jeremiah Beck came to the Chaparral as an Evangelical preacher from Indiana. Grandpa felt he was succeeding with God, but regarding earthly rewards, he looked like a failure. Visiting the local farmers for free dinners to persuade them to attend his house, he referred to as a church, was wearing thin the nerves of the local farmers. Had not their wives been sympathetic to Grandma Beck and their seventeen kids, Grandpa would have surely been asked to leave the Chaparral. Not one of Grandpa's fifteen boys followed in his footsteps as a clergyman. They skedaddled out of the Chaparral the day they graduated high school. After fifty years in the Chaparral, Grandpa and Grandma Beck came to own that little house turned church. It included two acres of property and sat on a gravely tree-covered hill next to a busy two-lane highway. Grandpa bequeathed an acre of his property to be a free Christian cemetery available at no charge to any believer.

Grandpa and Grandma died. The highway department widened the highway and condemned the little house-church, and the contractor walked a bulldozer through that little structure faster than a bolt of lightning. A problem arose with the Grandpa Beck Free Cemetery. By law, it could not be condemned and had to remain in perpetuity. In order to protect the inhabitants, and by law, the county became the trustee over the Grandpa Beck Free Cemetery. No funds were allocated for the upkeep of the free cemetery, no maintenance was done on the free cemetery, and so it sat, filled with

Grandpa Beck Free Cemetery

weeds, and overgrown with wild flowers and grasses. Every so often a guilt-ridden relative of one of the inhabitants would groom their resting place and plant a flower. But, as any common folk could see, the Grandpa Beck Free Cemetery laid in disarray and neglect. Local folks kept adding the dearly departed, yet not forgotten, to plots in the Grandpa Beck Free Cemetery. If a family was short on funds, the county poor farm administrator would suggest the Grandpa Beck Free Cemetery. My brothers Len and Garth Olson and I were attempting to grow the population of the Grandpa Beck Free Cemetery this very day.

In the Chaparral, there dwelled another family with seventeen kids. They were the Swartz. The Swartz were very nice folks who practiced the Hutterite religion, a self-sufficient group of hard workers who would lend a hand as long as the recipient was a believer and appeared to be trying. The Swartzs liked Grandpa Beck, and believed he was a righteous and believing man. However deep down, they held a quiet disdain toward Grandpa, thinking his talking and preaching all the time instead of working to provide for his family was a little too convenient. The Swartzs felt the idea that "God will provide" was being taken literally by Grandpa Beck.

The next to the youngest Swartz boy was named Jacob. He was a good-hearted lad and a hard worker. Problem with Jacob was his efforts were usually in the wrong direction. Not because he was on the wrong side of the law. Jacob was on the wrong side of smart. In an effort to provide firewood for the family, Jacob fell a seventy-foot tamarack tree across the Swartz barn that led to two milk cows being put down. Jacob went hunting one very late fall evening and almost in total darkness dropped the Faulk's prize bull thinking it was a deer. Jacob also burned a tick off the back of his elbow and dropped the match in dry grass resulting in a wind-driven fire that burned to the ground nearly ten acres of Swartz's stock feeding oats.

Jacob was reaching an age in Hutterite tradition when a young man found a good woman to cleave to, leaving the parental home. The Swartzs thought it best in Hutterite tradition that a fella

Hutterite marry a Hutterite lady but not one of your own relatives. Unfortunate for Jacob, the Swartz girls were mighty easy on the eyes. To solve the shortage of available marrying pairs, the Hutterites let it be known throughout the states where available suitors might be found.

Ruth Funk, from Terry, Kansas, came to live with the Monks in the Chaparral. The Monks, relatives of the Swartzs, were also a large Hutterite family and their daughter Ester went to live with the Funk family in Kansas. Of course, the idea was for these young ladies of marrying age to meet a fine upstanding Hutterite man and become wed.

God blessed Ruth with a kind heart, a solid work ethic, a quick smile, but not much else. Ruth was a large woman. No, it is better said Ruth was a very large woman. Ruth was fat. No again, it is better said Ruth was obese. She did not walk; she waddled. Her denim dresses drooped to the very soles of her size twelve shoes, and the top button of her denim shirt could not be buttoned without pinching her lowest chin. Ruth's face was as round as a basketball. Her skin was pale white except for her bulbous ruddy red cheeks. She wore glasses, always in need of cleaning, that hung halfway down her nose. The glasses could slide no further than her large flared nostrils. Ruth wore her hair in one very long braided pig tail that reached to her large protruding behind. A neat little crochet bonnet sat upon Ruth's head like all the Hutterite women wore when not working. A strong argument could be made that Ruth should shave her upper lip, but she did not.

All day Sunday and every Wednesday evening, the Hutterites congregated at their community-built church. Ruth sat with the Monks and Jacob sat in the Swartz pews. Soon the Monk pews were moved next to the Swartz pews, and Jacob found himself sitting next to Ruth. In reality, Jacob just sat there and looked at the floor. Ruth was the one who noticed and took great delight in sitting next to Jacob. Ruth made small talk toward Jacob and told him funny little stories to which he replied, "Uh-huh."

That very same year Ruth came to live with the Monks, old man Swartz went into the county seat and deeded ten acres of his home

Hutterite Church

place to Jacob. All the local Hutterites in less than three months built a plain, rectangular, dull, but efficient house with barn for Jacob on his land. Jacob and Ruth were then married in the Hutterite church and moved onto the ten-acre farm with the little house and barn. The wedding gifts for the newlyweds were chickens, rabbits, a cow, and a pair of breeding hogs along with the usual utensils, cookware, and linens.

Ruth started a large garden, milked the cow, picked wild berries, baked, canned, and provided a decent home life for Jacob. Jacob struggled. Old man Swartz gave him a D-6 Caterpillar tractor to get logging jobs. Then old man Swartz gave Jacob a Mack logging truck to help him along the way in providing for his family. Jacob did okay logging the local farmers' timbered land.

Then Jacob met my father, Horst Olson. They conspired to bid on a forest service logging contract and won the bid. Jacob was to haul logs to the Brewer's mill and Horst was to fell the trees, skid the trees with the D-6 Cat, and load the trees onto Jacob's Mack truck. Since Horst worked full time, his three sons were the labor force in the woods. Len fell trees. I skidded trees to the landing area using Jacob's D-6 Cat, and Garth bucked the trees on the landing and loaded them onto Jacob's Mack truck with a loader leased by Horst.

Sixteen hours a day we worked in the woods and Jacob delivered logs to the Brewer's mill, seventy miles away taking over four hours for a round trip. Jacob made as many as four trips per day. The logging operation made money. The cheap labor and the number of loads delivered to the mill daily were a financial success.

For two months things went fine with the logging operation, and then Jacob dropped down to no more than three trips to the Brewer's mill per day. Then Jacob was only making two trips per day. The logs piled up on the landing. When Horst came to work on the weekend, he was frustrated and grumpy.

Horst said, "Jacob, why in the world aren't you making four daily trips to the mill?"

Jacob and Ruth's Place

The D-6 Caterpillar

Being his nonchalant easy going self, Jacob responded, "Well it just takes that much time to make a round trip. We got to load the truck, unload the truck, get fuel, and of course the driving."

This response was not to Horst's liking. That very Saturday afternoon Horst followed Jacob on his second trip to the Brewer's mill. Horst stayed back so Jacob would not notice him tailing the logging truck. Jacob went straight way to Brewer's mill. He waited about a half an hour before getting unloaded, but upon exiting the mill, he turned the opposite direction from the woods and traveled ten miles to the Monk farm. He parked in a groove of trees on the county road and hastily crossed through the trees to the rear of the Monk farm house. All the Monk men were in the fields haying and ranching. He scrambled up some lattice on the side of the house onto the shed roof of the Monk kitchen and disappeared into an upstairs window.

Horst sat in his pickup truck waiting, curious but furious. Nearly one and one half hours passed before Jacob started his logging truck to get another load of logs. During loading on the landing, Horst confronted Jacob about his stop at the Monks when logs needed to be hauled. Jacob was calm and simply said, "I think I have found love. Ester Monk has returned home from Kansas because things had not work out for her. Ruth is a good woman, but I am in love with Ester Monk."

Horst scratched his head, looked at the ground, kicked at some dirt, and said, "Okay, I think I understand where you are coming from. But I am going to hire Jim Wills to help get these logs hauled. But, Jacob, you got to promise me you will do no less than three loads a day to the mill."

Jacob said, "Okay. I promise, but you gotta promise me that you will keep Ester and me a secret. You can tell no one!"

Horst nodded his agreement and they shook hands and both went their separate ways.

The summer ended and the forest service contract was complete. Horst became much better friends with Jim Wills than Jacob Swartz. They parted friends, but when other loggers asked Horst

JERRY HANSON

Loaded Logging Truck

about doing business with Jacob Swartz, Horst would reply, "Jacob's business seemed to be giving me the business."

That summer while at the Chaparral County Fair, the news came out that Ruth (Funk) Swartz had died. Rumor had it that she had miscarriage at home by herself and passed away. Everyone felt badly about Ruth. She was a kind soul. The next day on his way to church, Jacob Swartz dropped by Horst's house. With his hat in his hand, Jacob quietly asked Horst for a favor.

That is why Len, Garth and I with picks and shovels were at the Grandpa Buck Free Cemetery. We were hand digging Ruth's grave. We dug and dug on the hole until it was past dark. Gravel and sand slid back into the hole as fast as we could throw it out. A six-foot deep hole that was supposed to be three feet six inches by six feet six inches was only three feet deep and already over four feet wide by seven feet in length.

Horst arrived at the gravesite and accused us of slacking off! In unison we all replied, "You can't dig in this stuff. It keeps caving in."

Horst retorted, "They are bringing Ruth here tomorrow at noon, and we got to have this hole ready."

At six the next morning, we were back at Grandpa Becks Free Cemetery in Ruth's grave site hard at work. Horst went to see Gattor Brewer at Brewer's mill to ask him to donate some lumber to crib Ruth Swartz's every widening hole. Before Horst could return with the lumber, Ruth's future neighbor was slipping into the hole. We stopped and waited for Horst. Horst silently cursed, and we all got busy building a wood frame for inside the hole. Horst said, "We will just leave that other coffin as it is and move Ruth over about a foot. You boys keep your mouths shut about what's happened here. You got that!"

We dug feverishly, and the framework followed the digging into the hole. We filled in behind the timbers which covered up the neighbor next door. Right on time Ruth and the funeral procession turned off the highway at noon. The hole contained only five rows of twelve-inch timbers, and the top row stuck out of the ground seven inches. The hole was less than five feet deep. Hurriedly Horst said,

Not so Deep Gravesite

"Stop digging, dress up the hole and level off the ground, load up the leftover timbers, get the tools, and wait over there by the trees! Hurry along!"

We replied, "The hole ain't deep enough yet."

Horst replied, "Forget that. It's deep enough! You keep your mouths shut!"

From the trees in the back of Dad's pickup, we watched as the pallbearers brought Ruth to the gravesite. Following behind were the Monks, the Swartzs, Jacob and all the Hutterites and Ester. A nice short service was held at the gravesite. Then Ruth was lowered into the "not so deep" hole.

As the service broke up, Horst walked over to talk with Jacob and Ester. Horst quietly said something to Jacob.

Jacob nodded and said, "Okay."

Horst and Jacob shook hands. Horst then said to the boys, "If you've got all the tools, let's go."

We went to Brewer's mill and returned the timbers that were left over from the grave. Horst told Gattor Brewer that Jacob Swartz wanted to relay his thanks for the lumber donation.

Gattor said, "You got timbers left over?"

Horst replied, "We did not crib the bottom."

Gattor responded, "You are real lucky. We dig around here all the time and always have to crib right to the bottom of the hole."

Horst dropped the subject and said, "Yeah, well thanks, we got to be going. It's been a long day."

On the way home crowded into the pickup with streaks in the dirt on my face from sweating, I said, "Dad, don't we have to go back and cover up Ruth's grave?"

Horst grunted and said, "Nope, that's Jacob's business."

"Let us not get tired of doing what is right…"
(Galatians 6:9)

Jerry Hanson. 2017

HOWIE

When you were not old enough to get a paying job but too big to be under foot, there was not much to do in the summer time. We had spent the morning cutting corn from the cob. Mom was preparing it for canning. It was part of our winter food supply. When Mom started cooking in the kitchen, she told me, "You run on outside and play for a while. I don't want you hanging around this boiling water and hot stove."

I went outside and threw a tattered baseball off the barn roof and tried to hit it with a stick as it came down. Our neighbors, the Dailys, went by on the dirt road in their old pickup and beeped their horn and waved. We liked the Dailys, but they went up and down our dusty road all the time and beeped their horn at every house they passed. I thought they were just being friendly, but Mom and Dad said they were annoying. In a half hour, the Dailys went in the opposite direction and beeped again. I waived again. I was getting bored with my baseball game, so I went back inside to the kitchen.

I stood around until Mom seemed to not be so focused on canning corn and asked, "Can I walk down to Teddy's house and see if he can play?"

To my surprise, she said, "Yes."

I casually strolled down the dirt road passed the Wright's house, the Taylor's house, and the Zimmer's house. I kicked a few rocks along the way. The sun was high in the sky with a few scattered puffy clouds. There was no breeze. It was hot but not uncomfortably hot.

Country Road

I realized for some reason that every house I had passed was related to the Dailys. Even Teddy's family was related to the Dailys. The Sims and our house were the only houses on that mile of road not related to the Dailys. Actually, Mollie Daily was a Taylor girl and the Taylors had homesteaded in this area in the late 1800s. All the Taylor girls had married and never left the area. They had become Wrights, Zimmers, Lambs, Masons, Burfords, and Ferros. Two Taylor brothers had remained in the area. They feuded with each other and did not speak. Rumor had it that the older brother had married his sister after getting her pregnant. Their three kids were weird and everybody said they were inbred and crazy. I never saw them being crazy, but I knew they were reclusive and nobody visited or talked to them.

In a half mile, I turned down the lane to Teddy's house. Their car was gone. Their dog came out to greet me. He wagged his tail when I petted him. It looked like nobody was around, but I knocked on the door anyway. Whenever I knocked, the dog barked at me, but nobody answered the door. I waited a while. They had a foot scraper on the porch used for getting mud and manure off your shoes. I fiddled with the scraper and wiggled it to see how firm it was attached to the porch. It was pretty solid. The dog wandered off and I knocked again. Still no one answered.

I stood on the porch looking out at the corals and barn. I remembered last spring when Mom and Dad and my five brothers came to visit Teddy's folks in our old Hudson. The ground was sloppy because winter was trying to die. It would snow and then rain, and the rain would melt the snow. It made the ground sloppy and muddy. Teddy's dad had put down stepping stones from the lane up to the porch so visitors did not have to walk in the mud. As our Hudson came to a stop, I bolted from the rear seat nearest Teddy's house. I deftly skipped up the stepping stones to the porch before anyone else had exited the car. Teddy's mom was standing in the screen door smoking a cigarette. As she blew smoke through the screen door, over her shoulder, she said, "Vern! Here comes that pack of wild Indians."

I turned and looked out across the coral fences toward the barn and hills, studying the landscape for Indians. I saw none?

I knocked one last time but decided nobody was home. I figured they must have gone to town. I moseyed out their long driveway, stopping every so often to look at bugs or flowers. I picked some puff berries that grew on the bushes next to the lane. Puff berries are white berries about the size of your fingernails. A large puff berry is a little bigger than your thumb nail. Most of them tend to be more like the size of your little fingernail. Some kids called them pop berries, but my mom called them puff berries so that was what I called them.

The puff berry bushes were dusty. Cars driving on the dirt road kicked up lots of dust. It was late in August and most of these berries were large and puffy. I would pick several puff berries and put them on a rock in the road and stomp on them with my high top Keds. The berries would make a popping sound. The more berries I used the louder the pop. The bigger puff berries, I would throw as hard as I could against a rock and they would pop. I decided throwing was more fun and I could practice my pitching. It was pretty hard to hit some of the rocks in the road with the little berries. I figured that would even make me a better pitcher. Besides, there was an immediate umpire to call strikes. When I hit a rock, the berry popped. That was a strike!

I was pretty consumed with my puff berry game when somebody said, "Hey, whatcha doin?"

It startled me and I looked up to see this light brown-haired boy about my age and size looking at me. He wore a pair of blue pin-striped shorts with a belt and suspenders attached to the shorts. The suspenders went up over his shoulders. His shirt was collared and starched clean white. He was very neat. He wore a pair of sandals like shoes that strapped on his feet, yet his toes stuck out. He had on a pair of colored socks. His hair was neatly combed across his head with a large clump of hair in the front. I had never seen this kid before. Nobody in our neighborhood dressed like he did.

My old and worn white t-shirt had no collar. What collar it used to have was sagged and stretched out of shape. My t-shirt hung out the sides of my suspenders on my denim overalls. My overalls hit me about two inches above my high tops because I had outgrown them. I never wore socks. Mom had shaved my head at the start of summer vacation, and it was now about one-half-inch long all over. I never

Howard Russell Sinclair, III

combed it or had to comb it. It pretty much stuck straight out from my head. All in all, a pretty convenient summer hair style I thought.

I replied, "Poppin' puff berries."

He said, "Why you doing that?"

I said, "'Cause I want to and they pop." I stopped picking puff berries and we just looked at each other. Then I said, "Hey do you live around here?"

He replied, "We are on vacation at my grandma's place."

I said, "Who is your grandma?"

He responded, "My grandma's name is Lansbury and she lives over in that house." He pointed to a new modern flat-roofed house that sat near the creek with a view of the mountains. "She only comes here in the summer time to live."

I knew the house as the Sinclair house. It was always closed up and Teddy's dad watched it when it was empty. It was a much nicer house than any of the houses in our neighborhood. We had always heard somebody from back east had purchased an acre off the original Taylor homestead and built this new modern house.

I said, "I thought that was the Sinclair house."

He replied, "That's my name. My daddy owns the house, but my grandma comes out here to stay in the summer. We came this year to visit her on our vacation. My daddy just got here yesterday, but I've been here over a week. I leave tomorrow."

I said, "Why didn't your dad come when you did?"

He said, "He had to work. He flew to Portland and got a car to drive out here. My mother and I drove here, all the way from Washington DC."

He asked, "What's your name?"

I looked at him for a minute and then said, "Jimmy."

He said, "My name is Howard Russell Sinclair the Third. I am named after my daddy, but they call me Howie. You can call me Howie too."

Howie said, "Can I try to throw some of those puff berries?"

I replied, "Sure, I guess so. I snickered. I don't own the puff berries."

He picked some scrawny little puff berries and with his wrong hand threw them toward the ground. The berries flew up in the air because he let them go too soon. I looked at him kind of puzzled.

Howie said, "They didn't pop?"

I replied, "You gotta hit the rocks for them to pop! You didn't hit any rocks. In fact, you missed the road," I jeered.

Howie tried again and at least hit the road.

I said, "Howie, you gotta pick the big puff berries. They are easier to throw and they pop better. See!" As I flung a puff berry off a rock, it popped loudly.

Howie said, "That is neat."

Then from behind us, a deeper adult voice said, "Howard, it is time to come to the house."

There in Teddy's lane about thirty feet from Howie and I stood a tall dark-haired man in the nicest clothes I had ever seen. He was tall and slender. His shirt was collared and long sleeved, but he had rolled the cuffs part way up his arms. His pants were slacks and they fit loosely with cuffs at the bottom. He wore a shiny belt that matched his shiny shoes. He had this combed but bushy black hair with streaks of white or gray above his ears. He was handsome. I just looked at him.

The man continued, "We are going to the resort at the lake while it is still hot. I might take a swim. Come on now, Howard! Hurry along."

Howie said, "Hey, Daddy, can I invite my new friend Jimmy to come too?"

Walking away, Howie's father responded, "I don't care, just come on! We are going to leave."

Howie turned to me and said, "Jimmy, would you like to come along? The resort is lots of fun. We can go in the water, or skip rocks, or roller skate, and even get ice cream."

I knew all about the lake resort. I had been going there for years. It was a nice place for all the locals until some outfit bought it, fenced it, and started charging for people to come and use the beach. It was the best beach on the lake. They also built a roller-skating rink, made a campground, and built a snack bar. The best thing though, they

Resort Snack Bar

built a long wooden dock with a diving board and a floating wooden island off the end of the dock with a high diving board. I had jumped off both those diving boards. It was fun!

I paused for a minute as Howie pleaded, "Come on Jimmy! It is lots of fun."

Being the big-time puff berry pitcher I was, and since Mom was canning corn, and it was hot out, I figured I could make the decision to spend the afternoon at the lake resort.

I replied, "Okay, Howie, I will come along."

I stood silently next to this big Chrysler New Yorker with fins and white-walled tires. It was undoubtedly the best car our neighborhood had ever seen. Howie's father got in the driver's seat and an older lady got in behind him. Out of the Sinclair house rushed a pretty lady carrying a large basket with towels and other things draping from it. She was in a big hurry and turned to go back and lock the doors.

The older lady yelled from the back seat, "Charlene! You do not have to lock the doors here."

Howie's father said, "Come on, Charlene, let's go. Howie, get in the car and tell your friend to get in too. It is already nearly two o'clock and we are wasting the good sun."

Off we went down the road the five miles to the lake resort in the big Chrysler. Howie's father drove fast and lots of dust kicked up behind the big Chrysler. Mom would have really been mad about his driving. Road dust always got on her clean clothes, hanging on the line to dry.

At the lake resort, Howie's father paid the rate for a family with a car. Howie jumped out of the car when it rolled to a stop and said, "Come on, Jimmy. I will show you the dock."

Howie's mother said, "Hold it one minute, Howard. Introduce your friend to your grandmother and me, and you need to get some sunscreen on your face and arms."

Howie said, "Oh yeah, Mom and Grandma, this is my friend Jimmy."

I blushed and stood there as they both said, "Hello, Jimmy."

Howie's grandma then said, "You must be the Jensen boy?"

The Chrysler

I replied, "Yes, I am."

I wondered how she knew who I was. I stood there and looked at her. She smiled and looked back at me.

Howie's father had walked off to secure a picnic site with a fire pit and seats. Howie's mother had followed him to the site, but the grandma stood there, watching Howie and myself.

Finally Howie said, "Come on, Jimmy. Let's get to the lake."

The grandmother replied, "Howard, you go get your sunscreen on."

She turned to me and said, "Nice to meet you, Jimmy," and walked toward the barbecue site.

I stayed by the Chrysler while Howie got this white stuff rubbed on his skin. When he came back, we headed toward the beach.

Howie picked up a rock and said, "I can skip this rock off the water."

I looked down at the rock. Howie had selected a small completely round rock. I looked at Howie puzzled and said, "Howie, you need real flat rocks to skip off the water."

Howie just smiled and said, "Watch this."

With his left hand, Howie made a mighty gesture and the rock flew past my nose and bounced off a boat moored at the beach.

Howie said, "Oops," and laughed a little bit.

We spent almost one-half hour skipping rocks. I picked some rocks out for Howie, and he finally skipped a rock maybe one or two skips. I was fine with Howie. He was okay and pretty nice. I got to really practice my pitching with the rocks, and we also waded in the water to cool off. It was pretty hot out.

Then I said, "Hey, Howie, let's go out on the dock. We can jump off the diving board and swim to the island. Have you ever jumped off the high board?"

Howie just stood there with a funny look on his face. Then he said, "I can't go out on the dock or to the island."

I responded, "Well, let's go ask your parents."

Once again Howie had this funny look on his face and he looked down at his feet. He looked up and said, "I can't swim."

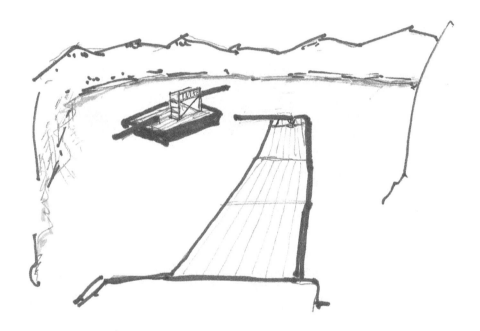

The Dock

Howie's father's voice interrupted us saying, "Come on, Howard. We are going to the barbecue place and get some food."

Howie said, "Can Jimmy come too?"

Howie's father said, "Does he have a dollar? It cost a dollar to eat."

Howie said, "Do you have a dollar, Jimmy?"

I got a funny look on my face and looked at the ground sheepishly and said, "No."

Howards father said, "Never mind him, Howie. Come along."

They walked off toward the camp site area and the barbecue. Howie skipped alongside his father and once turned and looked back at me. They disappeared into the camp site among the trees and the people.

I took off my shoes and went out on the dock. I sat on the dock with my feet in the water and looked back at the camp site. I figured Howie would finish and then come back to play. Two of the Daily kids were out on the island and said, "Hey, Jimmy, come on out. The water is great."

I usually love to swim, but for now I did not seem to want to swim. I replied, "Naw, I didn't bring my suit."

They smiled, waved, and said, "Watch this!" as they jumped off the high board.

After a while I walked up by the camp site and looked through the trees at the BBQ site where the Sinclairs were sitting. They were talking, eating, and playing cards. Howie was at a nearby site playing with two other boys about my age.

I walked back to the lake as the Daily kids were walking up the dock, wrapped in their towels.

I said, "Hey, are you guys leaving for home?"

They responded, "Yeah, we gotta go home."

I said, "Can I catch a ride home with you?"

They said, "Sure."

We all climbed into the back of their old pickup and headed out the gate for home. Mrs. Daily handed back a package of opened Red Vines through the pickup window as we started for home. As we went by the big Chrysler, I could see the Sinclairs having ice cream and Howie sitting with his new friends having ice cream too.

Red Vines

The Daily kids said, "Here, Jimmy. Have some Red Vines."

I was hungry and took two vines. They were good. I was quiet on the way home with the Dailys and didn't say much. Mom saw me get out of the pickup from inside our house.

As I entered the house Mom said, "You were gone to Teddy's quite a long time. I see you caught a ride home with Dailys."

As she spoke, I headed for the stairs to my room. I said, "Yeah, they were driving by."

I was about three steps up the stairs to my bedroom when I turned and said to Mom, "Do you know those people that live at the Sinclair place?"

She responded, "I met the grandmother at the school house on the Fourth of July. Why? Did you meet her?"

I replied, "Yeah, I kinda met her. There is a kid visiting there named Howie. I met him."

Mom said, "Oh, was he a nice boy?"

As I turned and headed on up the stairs, I responded over my shoulder, "Yeah, I guess he is okay. I think I like Teddy and the Dailys a lot better. He leaves tomorrow."

"Do to others whatever you would like them to do to you." (Matthew 7:12)

Jerry Hanson. 2018

CONSEQUENCES

Elvin Jackson was a tough black kid from Philadelphia. Elvin grew up in the hood. He was up and on the streets before the milkman made his deliveries. Elvin stayed out all day. He missed school and came home to a rundown apartment around midnight. He brought dumpster food home to share with his drunken mother. Elvin was not a big kid, but he was as smart as any street kid could be. He was tough. He had to be tough to survive. Kids in Elvin's neighborhood either fought bullies or paid for gang protection. Becoming part of a gang was not for Elvin. He stood his ground, and after a year's worth of bloodied noses, the bullies decided he was not worth their trouble. Elvin never looked for trouble, but trouble always found Elvin.

At fifteen, Elvin was arrested for being in front of a convenience store when it was robbed. He had nothing to do with the robbery. He was not part of the gang that pulled off the robbery. He did not hang out with the culprits and just happened to be at the store. The cops let Elvin go but put the incident on his record. Two years later, Elvin was riding his bike near a bank heist. The cops cordoned off the four square blocks around the bank. Elvin was inside the sequestered area. He was arrested and charged with accessory to the crime. The cops said Elvin was a lookout. Elvin had no legal representation and was sentenced to three years of confinement. Upon turning eighteen, Elvin was transferred from a youth correctional facility to the federal prison to finish his sentence.

Philadelphia

In prison, Elvin was immediately singled out, intimidated, and picked on. Two competing black gangs wanted Elvin as a member. Their idea of membership was for Elvin to become one of their underling service boys. The whites and Latinos did not want Elvin in their group and did not care what happened to him in prison. Elvin fought back. With speed and accuracy, he bloodied noses and cut eyes in yard fights. The fights landed him in solitary confinement. He found it safer and more comfortable in confinement. After numerous fights and when new inmates arrived at the prison, the gangs left Elvin alone. With few places to expend his energy, Elvin worked out in the prison yard and gym. He was not interested in becoming bulky or muscled. Street fighting had taught Elvin that speed, defense, and never getting hit were the keys to winning. He continually worked on agility, angles, and how to deliver quick, precise, and powerful blows while dodging punches.

Elvin entered a prison-sponsored boxing tournament. He easily won his weight division with four first-round knockouts. The inmates goaded the prison official to have the division champions fight for an overall prison championship. Elvin won matches over two other division champions and entered the overall championship bout. At 150 pounds, Elvin was one of the smaller division champions. As would be expected, Elvin had to fight the heavyweight champion in the final match. The heavyweight champ was a heavily tattooed, thirty-five-year-old muscular man, missing an ear who weighed 233 pounds. The fight was stopped in the fifth round before the man bled to death. Elvin danced, dodged, and landed fierce punches to the man's stationery head. The man's face was becoming swollen and red. The crowd booed Elvin and berated him for not standing and fighting. They jeered at him, "Stop running!"

Elvin continued his dancing and dodging, until the man bull rushed him and threw him to the mat. On the way down, the man tried to land his full body weight on Elvin. Elvin rolled out from under the brut and righted himself on his feet. The man struggled to his feet, and the referee tried to warn him to stop

Boxing

wrestling. The man brushed the referee to the side and charged across the ring at Elvin. As he approached, Elvin sidestepped him and threw a devastating left hook that split the man's nose wide open. Snorting and blowing bloody bubbles, the man careened off the ropes, and Elvin landed a triple combination on his right eye. The blows busted open a wide gash across his brow. The man's face was covered in blood. The ring was wet with blood. There was blood all over Elvin and the referee. The crowd was on their feet and cheering wildly.

The man staggered to his feet flailed wildly in Elvin's direction. Elvin unloaded another punishing left hook on the man's left eye. His left brow was now gushing blood. The man was a bloody mess. He could not see, and Elvin loudly said, "This fight is over. Get him some help!"

The man grunted and lunged in the direction of Elvin's voice, missing and falling face first into the mat. The referee signaled the fight was over and raised Elvin's hand in victory.

After the bout, Elvin was left to himself in the prison yard and gymnasium. No longer was he bullied into fights that sent him to confinement. Elvin's release date was nearing. He left federal prison on a sunny spring day. He had no plans for the future. With one set of street clothes and twenty dollars in his pocket, Elvin strode out the front entrance of the prison.

Outside the prison gate, a car was waiting. Elvin had made no arrangements to be picked up from prison. However, Jake: 'The Fixer' made sure he was in front of the prison when Elvin came out. Jake, with his best broad smile, offered Elvin a ride. Elvin got into Jake's Cadillac and said, "Thanks."

On the drive to town, Jake said, "Elvin, I have heard you are one heck of a boxer."

Elvin replied, "I don't think I really know how to box. I try to avoid fights, but it seems somebody is always picking a fight with me. I don't like getting hit, and I defend myself. That's what I have had to do in prison."

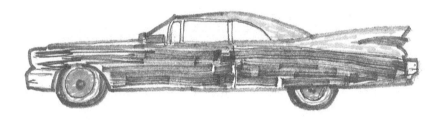

Jake's Cadillac

Jake said, "Well, I heard about the prison boxing tournament and how you came out on top. Have you thought what you might do on the outside? It is not easy out here for a convict."

Elvin responded, "I don't know what I am going to do. I have to find my mother and see how she is. Then I have to figure out how to make a living."

Jake left Elvin on a street corner in the slums of Philadelphia. Jake gave Elvin his business card and his phone number. Elvin found his way to his mother's old tenement building complex. It had been torn down. Inquiring around the hood, an old couple told Elvin his mother had been taken from the apartments in an ambulance over two years ago. Elvin slept on the street that night. It was damp, and he was cold and he shivered the whole night. The next day, he found his way to Jake's gym and walked in.

Jake 'The Fixer' became Elvin's boxing promoter. Elvin was given a room over the gym. Meals were arranged at a nearby diner for Elvin, and he was paid ten dollars per week to train as a boxer. Elvin never became a boxer. He was always a fighter.

After twelve fights, arranged by Jake, Elvin turned professional. Eight fights later, Elvin Jackson was ranked the number one challenger to the World Welterweight title.

Benjamin Parker was three years older than Elvin Jackson, but in worldly years, Elvin was much older. Benjamin was named by his great grandfather, a tribal elder who read the Bible incessantly. His grandfather, who he called Pops, liked the Bible story of Benjamin. Benjamin was born to a sixteen-year-old Indian girl out of wedlock. His mother left the reservation shortly after his birth and never returned. Benjamin was affectionately raised by his grandmother and her father. Benjamin was known on the reservation as Benji, and he lovingly called his grandmother Granny. Benji knew he was half Indian, but he always wanted to know who his father might be and how he got his greenish eyes.

Rumor around New Mexico had it that Benji's father was a Frenchman who hung around the bars in town and sold drugs on the reservation. His name was Perrot and not Parker. Benji

JERRY HANSON

Boxing Gym

not only had greenish eyes, he had a baby face. He liked to hang around the old men and Pops. They affectionately called him The Kid.

Benji did not attend school regularly. He went to school when sports were in season. Benji was an excellent athlete. Benji set school scoring records in basketball. He was an all-state wrestler for three years in a row and was an exceptional baseball player. Benji was unable to concentrate or focus on schoolwork. He was more interested in sports and the stories the old men and Pops told. He did not graduate.

One lazy hot summer day, Benji drifted into town. Although he was only eighteen and had a baby face, he decided to see if he could get served beer in a local bar. He strolled into the darken man cave and sidled up to the bar as if he was a regular patron. He sternly announced, "Give me a Bud."

The slovenly and grizzled bartender looked up at Benji and said, "Get the hell out of here, you dumb ass half-breed! In fact, get the hell out of town!"

Benji glared at the bartender and responded, "You ugly pig, go screw yourself the way everybody screws your mother!"

The bartender motioned to the bouncer to close the door as he strode around the bar. He said to Benji, "What did you say you little war-hoop?"

Benji responded with three hard punches to the bartenders face. It broke his nose which gushed blood. The bartender fell to his knees as the bouncer lunged at Benji. Benji deftly sidestepped the bouncer, and, as he went by, landed a solid right on his temple. The bouncer was out cold. Benji defiantly walked around the bar, grabbed a beer, took the cap off, and took a long swing. He belched and looked up just in time to see the bartender pull a Colt 45 from a drawer near the cash register. The bartender swung the pistol toward Benji. Benji quickly sidestepped the bartender's arm and pushed it away as the gun discharged. In the same motion, Benji broke the beer bottle over the bartender's head. The bartender groaned and fell to the floor. Benji "The

Indian Country

Kid" Parker stepped over the bartender and walked out of the bar.

The next day, the sheriff came to Granny's house with a warrant for Benji's arrest. The sheriff suggested to Granny that he become Benji's sponsor. He would try and keep Benji out of jail and prison. Granny did not fully trust white men or the system, but she knew Benji was in big trouble. The sheriff promised Granny and Pops that he would get Benji into some activities and training so he could function in society. Granny and Pops spent nearly an hour talking to Benji with the sheriff.

The sheriff finally said, "One way or another, Benji, I have to take you in. I have a warrant for your arrest. I can put you in custody, or you can come with me and I will try to help you. You decide."

The sheriff went out on Granny's porch to wait while Benji, Granny, and Pops talked.

In a few moments, Benji came out and said, "I have decided to go with you, Sheriff, and I would like you to help me out."

Two days later, Benji and the sheriff stood before a judge. With the agreement that the sheriff would be Benji's sponsor, the judge sentenced Benji to three years of probation and a one thousand dollar fine. Pops paid the fine for Benji, and the sheriff got Benji a part-time job at the gym and enrolled him in the Police Athletic League's activity programs.

Benji loved boxing and was soon the State Amateur Lightweight Champion. Benji realize, if you won titles, there was money to be made in boxing. The Indian Nation and the Police Athletic League were quick to put up money when Benji decided to become a professional boxer. In a three-year span, Benji won sixteen fights and fought for the World Lightweight Championship. He was quick, athletic, and had excellent knockout power. Benji, the Indian Nation, and the Police Athletic League were making lots of money on Benji's fights. The opportunity and an offer of more money came up if Benji would move up and fight for the World Welterweight Championship. Benji took the fight and the money. He won by a stoppage in the fourteenth round. However, Benji had both eyes cut,

The Roof

bruised ribs, and a broken left hand. It was a grueling fight. Because of television broadcast revenue, Benji had made more money than he could imagine. Benji was becoming wealthy, especially for a reservation kid.

The boxing organizations and promoters approached the Indian Nation and the Police Athletic League with a huge offer for Benji to defend his new title against Elvin Jackson. Benji was guaranteed three times more than he had earned in his title win. He jumped at the chance. He got what help and advice he could to quickly heal and went to work in the gym. The title match took place as scheduled. Elvin was naturally bigger than Benji and had more of a killer instinct in his arsenal. However, Benji's natural speed and athleticism neutralized Elvin's advantages. The fight was brutal and a crowd pleaser. Both fighters were knocked down in the fight but quickly recovered. With the crowd on their feet applauding both fighters, in the end, Elvin won a contested one-point split decision. Benji got a larger pay check, but he lost his title. A rematch was being planned by the promoters before the fight was over.

It had become a ritual at our house to watch the *Gillette Friday Night Fights*. It was Friday night, and the fights were on. The main event was the Jackson-Parker Welterweight Championship title rematch. I was up on the roof as the fight got underway.

Although it was late spring and we were experiencing a blizzard. It was cold, darker than dark, and snow was swirling as it fell. Gusting winds made my footing unstable, and I was nervous atop our two-story farmhouse. On the frozen, slick, highest, and steepest part of the roof, I was struggling to stand while turning the steel pole that held the four-foot aluminum television antenna. Dad was in the living room sitting in his worn fabric recliner awaiting the match. Dad would yell against the wind into the screen door, antenna turning directions to my brother, Glen. Glen would relay the directions up to me. "Back to where you were!" "That's better, hold it there!" "You lost it again!" Glen would repeat.

Mom's Popcorn

Sometimes, I could hear Dad's voice first, usually sounding angry, because I could not keep the fight signal in place.

I stuck my fingertips in my mouth, placed them into my hand, and then blew into my hand. For an instant, it helped the stinging frostbite. Then my fingers just went numb. Back on the pole, my hands stuck to the steel. Turning the pole with one hand made for treacherously poor footing, but I could put my numb hand into my pocket. A gust of wind almost took me off the roof! I settled for two hands on the pole.

Then I heard, "For Pete's sake! I'm missing the fight. Do I have to come up there and do everything myself?" said Dad.

"What the heck are you doing up there?" Glen chimed in.

I got busy again, forgot my fingers, shaky footing, and started searching in the dark for the right antenna position. For a few rounds, the reception was OK.

In the quietness of dark, I began to wonder. Why was I on the roof? I loved the *Friday Night Fights*. Mom made the best popcorn with lots of salt and butter. Watching the fights was one of the rare things we did with Dad. My oldest brother, Len, was sitting down there right now taking in the fight with Dad. Even Glen could watch the fight through the screen door! It was better freezing to death looking through the screen door watching the fight than freezing to death and falling off the roof into the night with no fight.

A roar went up in the living room. Something had happened in the fight.

"What's going on?" I asked.

There was no response. Apparently, Glen had gone inside.

In cold silence, I was left with my thoughts. Nine months earlier, when the dirt roads were dusty and not snowy slick, Mom and Dad went into town to Monkey Wards and bought a fifteen-inch Airline metal box television which was down in the living room. It came with a set of useless rabbit ears. We were the first family on that windy three-track dirt road to have television. We were excited, proud, and felt important in the neighborhood.

Airline Television

Von Trimble was in my grade at school. He was nearly a year older than I. He was bigger and a bully. Von was a show off and liked to draw attention to himself at others' expense. He loudly stated to me, in front of everyone at school, "You won't get any good TV reception because the closest station is 150 miles away."

I hated that wise guy know it all. He always ridiculed us, and it even angered me more that he was usually right. If we challenged him, he got our teacher, Mr. Rollins, to back him up.

The rabbit ears on the TV gave us ghost's images hidden in this black and white matrix of dots. At 9:00 p.m. nightly and sometimes earlier, we got a test pattern on the TV. The test pattern was bright and clear as a bell. I always thought if they can broadcast a good test pattern, why can't they broadcast better program reception?

Dad started checking around on how to get better reception. Soon, we had to stop bragging to the neighbors that we had TV. In fact, all we had was snow! And not just on the roof. Dad asked all his acquaintances and associates that would listen, "How can I improve my TV reception?"

None of Dad's friends or acquaintances owned televisions. None of them knew a darned thing about televisions! Televisions were brand new! Nobody else had a TV in our area! At a school play, Von's old man loudly chuckled and said, "You should have checked on reception before you bought a TV!"

He laughed. I was mad. His old man was just as much a wise guy as Von!

Somewhere, Dad heard of the possibility of pointing an aluminum antenna toward the direction of Buck's Mountain, where a signal repeater was located. Buck's Mountain was hardly a mountain, but it was geographically located near Lake Fortune. The open space created by the lake allowed for a fairly good broadcast signal. There were lots of things we could use more than a TV around our house, but we had a TV, and now we needed better reception. Dad was going to solve this problem, and off he went one Saturday morning and came home with a four-foot aluminum antenna. The next day, from the scrap heap behind the barn where Dad kept

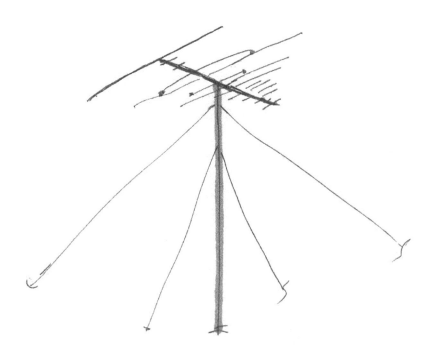

TV Antenna

his pilfered construction materials, we found a nine-foot long steel pipe. Dad, who was quite clever as a craftsman, rigged up a connection to hold the antenna on top of the pipe. That weekend, my brothers, my Dad, and I were up on the steep roof placing guy wires in four directions to hold the steel pole in place yet allowing it to turn.

The reception was better when the antenna pointed east toward Buck's Mountain. The antenna could also be turned 180 degrees, and sometimes, the reception was better. There were lots of antenna options for reception. The reception was never great, but it was better than rabbit ears. Again, we put the word out: "We have TV!"

I thought I heard the door shut, but it was hard to tell in the blizzard. I did not feel my fingers anymore, and I began to recall how KLTV Television, over one hundred miles away, had a kid's show on right after the evening news. We always ate supper with the evening news on TV. Mom's back was to the TV, but Dad had the prime chair. My chair was not great, but I could look sideways and see TV. This kid's show had a rag tag puppet that said corny things and made the dumbest jokes. They called him Houndog. Just before school started, KLTV had a contest to find Houndog a permanent name. You could win some cool prizes at the Monkey Wards and Gambles stores if you entered a name and it was chosen. I wanted a bicycle, the top prize, but a fishing pole would be all right too. For three weeks, I thought and thought about a name for that puppet.

Houndog was black and white, ragged, with floppy ears, a long nose with a black tip, and a big black circle around his right eye.

"I got it! Spot! Yes, Spot was the perfect name for that puppet."

They were going to award three places. Spot should get me into the top three. I never thought I was perfect at things, but I was quite sure that usually I could get into the top three. Mom helped me craft my entry letter and address the envelope. I got a stamp, put it in the mail box, and put up the red flag.

Rural Mailbox

Len and Glen said, "You're wasting your time. Spot will never win. The city kids will come up with better names." And, "You know, the city kids have parents that work at the station, they will win!"

The contest was ending at the end of the week, and now I was concerned if my entry got to KLTV on time. The naming contest buildup continued nightly on the show, and my delivery concerns mounted. Then Friday night came, and they announced the winners. The top three people all selected Houndog as their name!

My brothers laughed. Mom looked at me, and Dad said, "Well, that does make sense."

I wasn't mad or upset. In fact, I thought Houndog was the better name, but it should have gotten first place and that left room for spot in second or third. Oh well, maybe my entry never got there in time anyway. I was glad I never said a word to Von. A gust of wind hit me, and I grabbed the antenna pole. It swayed and spun, but it kept me on the roof.

I heard Dad yell out, "What happened to the signal?"

I righted myself and yelled back, "Is that better?"

It was, and he said, "Oh, you can come down. Didn't your brother tell you the fight is over?"

The fight was vicious. Elvin Jackson beat on Benji Parker, and then Benji beat on Elvin. Late into the fight, Elvin Jackson trapped Benji "The Kid" Parker on the ropes, pummeled him, and knocked him out.

Ten days later, while eating supper and watching our TV, it was announced that Benji "The Kid" Parker, former Welterweight Champion of the world, had died from head injuries he received in the fight.

It was real quiet at the table.

Dad said, "Benji was a real good fighter."

A week later, as I ambled my way home from school, it sunk in that I had missed the fight because I was on the roof! Why wasn't Glen or Len on the roof? I decided that my bragging about climbing skills to Dad in front of my brothers is what put me on the roof. I also reached the conclusion: Von reacted after I did some eye-catching thing or made a comment that made me look cool. I might be

JERRY HANSON

Houndog

166

the cause of some of my own circumstance. I vowed to myself that very day on that old dirt road, "It was time to take charge of my own actions!" Hereto forward, I would take cause and affect into account with my decisions! If I was ever going to amount to much, I had to get smarter or suffer the consequences! I figured smart choices would allow me to become somebody, someday. I could be a doctor or a lawyer. I might even be famous or rich. Making good choices was paramount. Benji should have made better choices.

"....how does a man become wiser? The first
step is to trust in the Lord!" (Proverbs 1:7)

"A fool gives full vent to his spirit, a wise man
quietly holds back." (Proverbs 29:11)

Jerry Hanson. 2017

FIGURES

Our souls may be defined by our virtues or lack of virtues, but the physical world defines us by what we have or do not have. This conundrum exists for both men and women. In today's environment, a man may deal with virtue differently than a woman. But success for both hinges not only on their capabilities but on their chosen behavior. The workplace is ripe with challenges against our virtues and morals. The workplace is where most acquire the resources necessary to obtain material holdings. For most, the workplace is a continual struggle. Owning a refreshing and beautiful pool in your backyard for use on a hot summer day can be a tangible delight for the total family. The rewards for exemplary moral character and stellar virtues may never yield a backyard oasis. You can ponder the outcome of living a moral life or you can take a cool dip.

Camilla Hoyt-Garza was facing such a dilemma. She turned out the lamp on the bedside table, pulled the covers up under her chin, and said goodnight to her husband Roland whom she called Rollie. Rollie had already fallen asleep on his side of the bed. For fifteen years, Rollie and Camilla had worked hard, been good neighbors, attended church, and volunteered in the community. Still they struggled to make ends meet. They drove old cars, the sun-damaged paint on the house suffered from lack of maintenance, the backyard did not have a pool, and the girls needed new clothes for the private school they attended. Silently in the dark, Camilla looked at

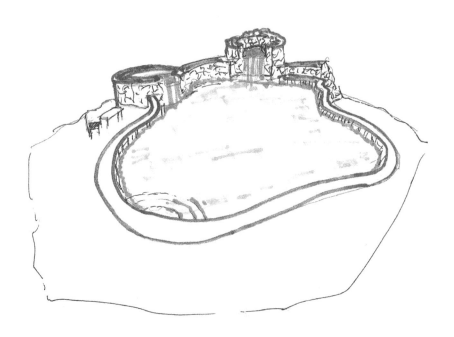

Swimming Pool

the ceiling and silently asked the Lord for his blessing and to make everything work out well, come Monday morning.

When it was discovered sunlight could be converted to electrical energy, the carbon-burning utility companies and their stockholders' nerves were on edge. Engineers huddled with financial gurus to prove the new source economically feasible. Marketing whizzes scrambled to see how this new technology could be sold and who would be in the best position to sell it. Boards paid exorbitant consulting fees to analyze the effect on the balance sheets. Environmental activists were filled with glee and Camilla Hoyt-Garza got a boob job, an enhancement that could rival any application of silicon panels to a dormitory rooftop.

It is happenstance that silicon has two such distinct but separate applications. Camilla had an average face, in general a nice figure and plenty of brains, just not enough boobs. On Monday morning at 8:00 sharp, Camilla had an interview with Resource Energy. She stood in front of her full-length closet mirror at 6:30 a.m. It was decision time. The tight red sweater with the pointy uplifting bra underneath or the scooped-out V-neck and slinky bra beneath. Camilla knew her choice was critical. How should she appear to the power players at Resource Energy? Using the rationale that a job interview might not be a format for too much skin, Camilla chose the red sweater. Camilla had been around the work world long enough to know the sweater would offer as much as her face or resume did, at the interview.

Bill O'Malley, Jace Eddy, and Grey Jackson joined one another with Camilla's resume in the conference room. Bill directed an assistant to bring them coffee, and a discussion began regarding the need to reach community college directors and school board members to get them to install solar energy on their campuses. Bill was a financial expert and had brought the venture capital together to form Resource Energy. Jace was an accomplished energy engineer with a legal background, and Grey was a marketing genius. Grey was one of those bright young individuals who capitalize fully on his minority status. It had gotten him into the best universities and help land the best paying jobs, and public institutions gave favorable treatment

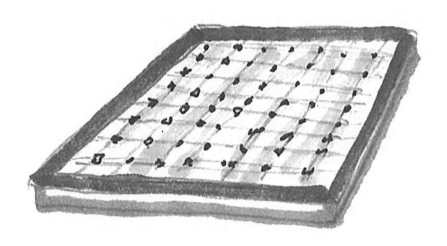

Solar Panels

when Grey was visible in the project selection and awarding process. The California School agencies had millions of capital improvement dollars to spend on facilities. The public was primed for clean energy projects and minority participation within the projects. However, too many boards and school administrators tended to fund student demanded rest areas, open spaces, safe spaces, and coffee shops in lieu of energy projects. Campus energy bills averaged in tens of thousands of dollars monthly. Resource Energy audits recommending equipment retrofits combined with solar energy cut those costs in half. Renewable energy grants, tax incentives, and the political popularity of clean energy made these projects a win for everyone involved. Resource Energy had the figures. The difficulty was getting the right people with the right figures in front of the decision makers. Public decision makers keep their lofty positions by avoiding decisions, taking no chances, not even calculated risks.

Lawyers lurked in the wings awaiting any type of legal funding violations or administrative missteps. The bureaucracy had become paralyzed while the possibilities for projects were unlimited. Glad handing and insincere elected officials, power-seeking political appointees, inept equality hires, and the bulging bureaucracy were difficult to get past. Boxes of doughnuts and specialty coffee got left on secretary's desks. Resource Energy needed to solve this puzzle, and they were interviewing in search of the right candidate to hopefully provide that solution.

Camilla, decked out in her tight red sweater, confidently delivered smooth answers to every question Bill, Jace, and Grey asked. With ease, she landed the job. Camilla became the public agency account executive for Resource Energy starting immediately. Camilla had never had a salary close to the two hundred thousand the job paid. Camilla also had never had a position that included all benefits fully paid, an open-ended expense account, and an elegant company car. The frosting on the cake was a two-and-one-half-percent commission paid to Camilla on her gross sales. This afternoon she would put in for two weeks leave from her current job starting tomorrow and at the same time give notice of quitting. If there was a problem, she would simply demand to be paid off. One way or another

RED

Red Sweater

she would be on the payroll at Resource Energy starting tomorrow. On the way home, Camilla smiled in her rearview mirror, giggled in delight, and pinched her leg to make sure this was not a dream. It was not. Resource Energy was real. The company was pleased too, but Jace Eddy was guarded until Camilla provided tangible results.

Although Bill had little use for the environmental activist groups, Jace and Grey convinced him to expend several hundred thousand dollars in donations and contributions to the environmental and renewable energy activist groups. They were banking on the activists stirring up public awareness and political pressure to shed light on the benefits of renewable energy. Resource figured with public awareness, their engineering and financial figures, and Camilla now making contacts and getting audiences, the doors into energy projects with the school districts would be swinging open.

Camilla stood tall and elegant in her patent leather high heels, a knee-length snug skirt, and a loose-fitting silk plunging V-necked blouse near the secretary's desk and in front of the superintendent of schools office. As she heard the doorknob to his office begin to turn, with practiced precision and purpose, she dropped her business card on the floor. The door opened and Camilla, as gentile and ladylike as possible, stooped down as practiced to retrieve the card. The plunging neckline of her blouse opened ever so slightly, just enough that her full bosoms, snuggling in her bra, left little to a male's imagination.

Simultaneously the superintendent bent down to rescue her business card. Facing one another, both the superintendent and Camilla paused, her looking at his face and him glancing lower. They rose up simultaneously. Her figure could not be ignored and his eyes never met hers, until she said, "Hello."

Then he cleared his throat and said, "Hello, my name is Bob Groves." Introducing himself as the superintendent of schools," he warmly extended his hand.

"Hi." Camilla demurred. "I'm sorry. I am so clumsy with these new cards. I'm Camilla Garza. I know it is almost quitting time, but I wanted to leave an energy brochure and some figures with your office today. I left some figures earlier with Mr. Knowles and Mrs. Clayton of your school board."

Camilla's V-Neck

"Oh, I see? Well, okay," replied Bob. "I can take your brochures and figures also. Why don't you come into my office. I have a few minutes."

He turned and said to his secretary, "Evelyn, you can go ahead and go home. I can take care of Miss Garza. It won't take long." He then said to Camilla, "Well, Miss Garza, come into my office and let's take a look at your figures."

Camilla spent almost an hour with Bob Groves going over the Resource Energy brochures, energy calculations, and cost saving figures. The meeting was friendly and the superintendent told Camilla to call him Bob. He even gave her the names of two other gentlemen on the school board for her to visit. He volunteered to set up the introductions for her, which later he did. Camilla met with both Mr. Richmond and Mr. Anderson, going over figures with each of them, leaving brochures for their use, and discussing possible projects. Camilla took each of them to dinner at the finest restaurants, on the Resource's expense account.

Camilla was pleased and reported her inroad successes to Bill and Grey who passed the progress on to Jace.

Camilla invited Bob to attend a professional baseball game in the company's box seats. Bob declined but apologized. He then suggested they go to dinner.

Bob said, "I might have a surprise for you."

A time for dinner was set. Camilla wore a brand new scooped out evening dress, had her hair done up, and armed with her company charge card headed off to dinner with Bob at the Orleans Steak House in the Redstone Hotel. This was the finest restaurant in the city. The evening went well with small talk about the school district, political personalities, the project decision process, renewable energy in the public sector, budgets, and possible savings.

Bob then leaned in close to Camilla and softly said, "I think I can get your company on the board agenda for some major projects."

Camilla giggled and said, "Oh, Bob, that would be so appreciated. What can I ever do to thank you?"

Bob responded, "Well I am free for this evening. If we could find somewhere comfortable, we could discuss the possibilities further."

Room Key

Camilla said, "I only have a couple hours before I need to pick up my daughters from their dance class, but Resource Energy has a suite here. We could continue our dialog there."

Camilla arose and placed a plastic key near her plate on the table and said, "Seventieth floor, Suite A. Give me a few minutes, Bob."

Camilla freshened up in the room, removed her undies and bra, sprayed an elegant perfume across her bosom, and placed her jewelry in her purse. She dimmed the lights, turned on the stereo speakers, and poured herself a glass of white wine from the bar. She knew Bob would not be too long, and it couldn't take more than an hour before she was off to pick up the girls.

There was a knock on the door and Camilla opened it slightly.

With a throaty gush, she said, "Please come in, Bob."

Bill, Jace, Grey, and Camilla each brought their figures into Resource Energy's conference room at 8:00 a.m. sharp. Resource had been awarded one hundred and thirty nine million dollars of energy work with the school district to be constructed over the next two to six years. Camilla's full 2.5 percent bonus was worth nearly three and one half million dollars. This meeting was to advise, discuss, and review the legal requirements in Camilla's employment contract. It was correct that her contract allowed for up to 2.5 percent of her gross sales. However, there were some restrictions. The commission percentage decreased as projects exceeded five million dollars. Also commission percentage diminished with multiple contracts or contracts with the same client. Bill, Jace, and Grey wanted to be fair, but they were not going to freely pay over three million dollars in bonus commissions. Furthermore, they advised Camilla that her commissions regardless of percentages were maxed to equal no more than one calendar year's salary. If the school projects lasted the full six years, Camilla commissions could reach over one million dollars. However, if the projects could be completed in one year, her commission would be two hundred thousand dollars.

The discussion began to focus on when and what years the projects were to be initiated, when the project would be complete, and how Camilla's commissions would be computed. Jace had the responsibility of design and construction schedules. Grey interfaced

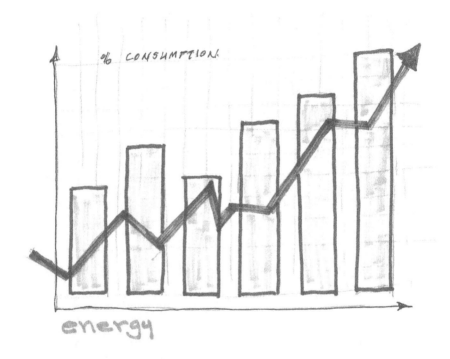

Energy Figures

with the clients for schedule coordination and access. But, Bill had the final authority over personnel and payments.

Camilla approached Bill as they retrieved a doughnut and some coffee. She wore a loose fitting but revealing white cashmere sweater. As she reached for sweetener, she brushed elegantly against Bill's arm.

Camilla said, "Doesn't it seem possible that after all my efforts to land those school jobs, that you all could schedule the projects to effectively span six calendar years instead of one or two years? I would think you, as accomplished businessmen, could figure something out." Turning and standing very close to Grey, Camilla said, "I think I could get us at least two more large jobs with this school district. Do you think you could get Jace to schedule our current work to span over six calendar years?"

Bill looked at Jace and said, "What do you think, Jace? Can't we work something out for Camilla? I don't know what she did or how she did it, but I must admit, her performance was beyond expectations. We had nothing with this district until she sold these projects."

Jace turned to Bill and Grey and said, "I am so glad and delighted we got these projects. I am pleased at Camilla's efforts. But you both know we spent big bucks on the activist, the politicians, and for media hype. These schools were ripe for renewable energy projects. Nothing against you Camilla, but most likely a decent salesman could have probably landed most of these projects for us."

Camilla demurred and shyly looked at the floor.

Jace's face turned slightly red and he turned and looked at Camilla. He said, "If I could get a good feeling about contract activation dates and construction schedules, I suppose over a six-year span, you would qualify for over a million dollars in commission. Or if we expedited these projects forward, we could get them done in a couple years. That is nearly a one-million-dollar difference in commissions. Camilla, that is a considerable amount of money for this company to pay out. I must consider the company and our other employees. I surely hope you can understand my concerns."

Camilla blushed, uneasily shifted her weight on her feet, and continued looking down at the floor.

JERRY HANSON

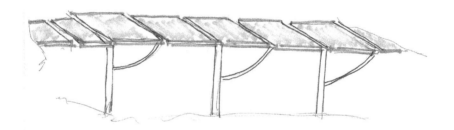

Renewable Energy Projects

Bill interjected and said, "Well, Jace, you are the one that sets up the contracts and schedules. I am very happy with Camilla's efforts, and I will be happy with whatever you decide and however you proceed."

Bill glanced over at Grey and continued, "I'm comfortable leaving this decision to be worked out between Jace and Camilla. What do you think, Grey?"

As Grey paused, Jace interjected, "Before anything can be resolved, I need to meet with engineering and construction and see what our commitments and obligations are. Maybe we could all meet again in a couple days after I see how those schedules work out."

Grey responded, "Bill, Jace, I am completely fine with this work getting scheduled over the next five or six years, especially if Camilla can get us more jobs. Bill, since you seem okay with this, I suggest Camilla meet with Jace, ease his concerns, and figure this out."

Bill said, "I agree, Grey. Jace, why don't you meet with engineering and construction and then set something up with Camilla this coming week. Just let Grey and I know your decision."

Jace said, "Fine."

He turned to Camilla and said, "What does your schedule look like over the next week or so?"

Camilla replied, "I need to be downtown next week. We could meet at the Orleans around three in the afternoon on Thursday, if that would work for you?"

Jace said, "Good, let's just make that work. Let's do it!"

Driving home effortlessly in the company car, Camilla thought of what she would wear to her meeting with Jace. The neighbor's girls were also in dance, and her neighbor would be picking up on Thursday. Rollie was on a long-haul job in the Midwest, so Camilla was free until 9:00 p.m. come Thursday. With these commission bonuses, they would buy a bigger house, move to a better neighborhood, put in a large swimming pool, get two new cars, and even start college funds for the girls.

As she exited the freeway, she silently said to herself, "Hmmm... did Jace go for the tight red sweater or does he respond more to visual openness?"

JERRY HANSON

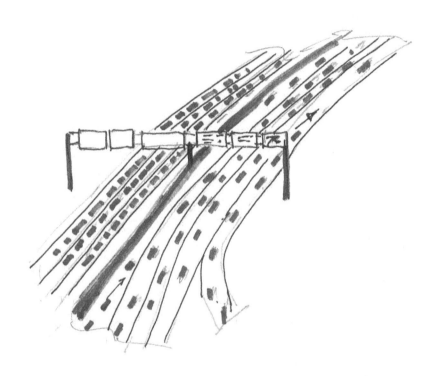

Freeway

Camilla pinched herself once, then twice more on the leg. Then she pinched herself hard.

She said aloud to no one, "Can this be real? Thank you so much, Lord! Amen!!"

She answered herself even louder, "Yes! It is real! Camilla Hoyt-Garza, my girl, can you believe the modern uses of silicon!"

"And how do you benefit if you gain the whole world and lose your soul in the process?" (Mark 8:36)

Jerry Hanson. 2019

BIG GAME

For five days snow had fallen in the Northwest. It was heavy and wet. For early November, this was unusual weather. The county road graders could not keep the rural roads plowed. There was simply too much snow and too many miles of road to plow. Our road to town and the outside world was no longer passable. We were snowed in. The local radio station was broadcasting road conditions and the status of school bus routes. Our school bus would not be running until further notice.

After brushing the snow off my coat and hat and hanging them in the coat room, I sat down and took off my wet boots. Then, I came inside our modest farm house. I had been splitting wood for our stove. We had plenty of wood, but the amount split was running low. From outside the house, I filled the wood box with all it could hold.

The house was cozy and warm and had a wonderful smell from Ma's cooking. Ma had started a kettle of stew that morning. It was still simmering on the stove, and the odor was throughout the first floor of our house. Ma made the best stew from elk meat we had hunted and vegetables she canned that summer from her garden. The stew was delicious especially with Ma's warm home-made bread and butter.

It was late afternoon and I had to help the Wertzs feed and milk their cows. Bud Wertz had gone to a funeral in Dawson county and could not return home until the roads were reopened. Ma had made

Home-Made Bread

my dinner early so I could leave and help Mrs. Wertz and the Wertz girls complete their farm chores.

Eating my stew, I recalled the hunting trip that provided the elk which was now in Ma's stew. In rural farm country, most folks had small self-sufficient places. Like most rural families, my family hunted deer and elk during fall hunting season. We stocked up our freezers with meat for the winter. Some families raised hogs and cattle for their meat. My family did both, but it was a family rite and tradition to hunt, especially for big game.

Pa was an excellent hunter and marksman. My older brother, Lewis, had become even a better hunter and marksman. Lewis simply always got his game and never missed a shot. My other brother, Fred, was a better hunter and marksman than I. In our part of the country, I was no better than an average hunter. I did not care. Sometimes I thought I didn't like killing the animals. I think I flinched on purpose when they were in my sights. That is something I would never admit to Pa or my brothers.

Uncle Wally Walker had a ranch in the Eagle Valley. His ranch was much larger than our place but considered small for a cattle ranch. Wally had six hundred acres that spanned the valley from the Eagle River to the base of the Eagle Range. His ranch was surrounded by miles and miles of federal forest service land. Under a permit, Wally grazed his cattle in the summer on US forest service land. The Eagle Valley and the Wally's ranch were beautiful but very remote.

Pa bumped into Wally at our regional feed store. Wally told Pa the Eagle Range elk herd had migrated down from the peaks into the valley because of heavy mountain snowfall. The following weekend we were going to Wally's ranch and hunt elk. In the early morning we left home in the dark. The seventy-mile trip on slick snowy roads took nearly two hours. We arrived at 7:00 a.m. As usual, the Walkers were up and had completed their morning ranch chores. Wally's and his boy Will had been down in the meadows the day before. They had some bad news about the elk.

The government-protected wolf pack had attacked the elk herd and killed a yearling calf. The bad news was the wolf pack had scattered the elk herd into groups of four to a dozen or so. The elk were

Timber Wolf

on the move and probably headed back into Eagle Peaks to escape the wolves. If we wanted to hunt elk that weekend, it would not be down in the valley. Pa and Wally decided they did not want to go into the mountains hunting but thought the boys should go ahead and see if they could cross, any tracks and possibly get an elk.

Will was the same age as Lewis, Will was six foot three and Lewis was five foot eight. Lewis was a far better athlete and woodsman, but Will felt his size made him boss. Lewis recognized they were in Walker territory and let Will push his way around. Fred and I fell into our proper place and followed along doing our part when required.

We got into the Walker's farm jeep and headed up Eagle Highway. In ten miles, we crossed Lion Creek, and Will stopped the jeep. He said, "The Miller boys told me elk tracks crossing the road were seen in this area. The elk would be heading into the clear cuts at the base of the Eagle Peaks or even headed back up into the mountains."

Lewis got out of the jeep and said, "I'm going to check around the roadside for tracks."

He crossed the Lion Creek bridge and walked along the side of the road. He carefully studied the ground in the barrow pits, the shrubs, and in the roadway. He motioned us forward and loudly said, "These tracks are fresh! And, most likely only a few hours old. The elk are on the run and there are wolf tracks following."

Will, Fred, and I got out and looked at the tracks. Will agreed. Lewis and Will decided to follow a logging trail up Lion Creek into the clear cuts hoping we might come across the elk or their tracks again. In about four miles elk tracks crossed the logging road, heading for a shallow canyon that lead straight into the steep Eagle Peaks. The tracks were fresh, but there were no wolf tracks following.

We parked the jeep and got all our gear together. I had long wool socks inside my rubber pack boots with long underwear and heavy woolen pants. We wore layered warm shirts under our red plaid coats and red stocking hats. It was cold and the snow was falling in tiny frozen ice particles. Visibility was less than seventy-five yards. I had my 30-30 Winchester rifle, my skinning knife, some

JERRY HANSON

Model 94 30-30 Winchester Rifle

rope, extra bullets, a sandwich, and a two Baby Ruth candy bars. We all had about the same dress and provisions.

Off we went following the elk tracks toward the shallow canyon. After crossing the clear-cut area, we entered an area of downed trees. The trees had been hit by a rare tornado and lay in a crisis crossed pattern, like God had dumped out a box of toothpicks. It was a maze and very difficult to traverse. The elk seemed to stride over or jump the downed trees. We either rolled over them or ducked under them. We came to the West Fork of Lion Creek and carefully waded it, avoiding deep holes. As we were coming out of the creek bottom, Lewis held up his hand and quietly but firmly said, "Stop."

We stopped and motionlessly held our position. Lewis slowly raised his rifle and fired a shot to the side of us. The brush exploded as a pack of at least ten wolves bolted away from us into the woods.

Will said, "Holy cow! They were close!"

Then he turned and scolded Lewis, "You know those wolves are protected as an endangered species. We can get in a lot of trouble just threatening them."

Lewis said, "I knew what I was doing! I shot over them to get them out of here. They lost the elk scent in the creek bottoms and are circling to pick it up again. We need to drive them off. The elk will never settle down if the wolves are running them."

We marched on. I was in the trailing position and began to nervously watch for wolf eyes behind us.

In a half mile we came to the base of the small canyon that led into Eagle Peaks. The Peaks shot three thousand feet straight up off the valley floor into the sky. They seemed very high because they were steep and had no foot hills. There were routes to the south that migrated through high elevation valleys and onto ridges, allowing a more gradual and steady climb into the peaks. Those routes were longer and took more time to get to the top. The fastest way up the peaks was straight up the rock slides in and out of the cliffs. It was slow going and you had to be careful, but it was by far the fastest way to the top.

It was now nine thirty and it was still snowing icy particles. After looking up at the Peaks, Lewis said, "Well, Pa brought us out this week-

JERRY HANSON

Eagle Peaks

end to get our game. We only have two weekends left to hunt before the season closes. I guess we better see if we can get an elk or two."

Will said, "Those elk are now running again and we will never catch up to them. They won't stop until they think the wolves have given up. I don't see any way to get to them."

Lewis said, "Well Will, what if we go straight up the rock slides and get to the top plateaus where they summer, just about the time they do?"

Will said, "Well last summer, Danny Miller and I climbed up to the plateau just about where we are now. I'll bet the elk are headed there. The wolves will give up before they ever go up there. The elk can handle this snow better than the wolves."

Up the rock slides and into the cliffs we went. It was soon apparent we all had to be on different routes since rocks, snow, and debris from the person above would careen into those following. I ended up way out on the left flank of our group. Soon we were in the clouds and visibility was less than fifty feet. I could see Lewis next to me, but I could not see Fred or Will. Slipping, sliding, and carefully placing our feet in carefully made footholds, up into the Eagle Peaks one foot at a time we climbed.

After hours of climbing, I was facing the base of a sheer cliff that shot up into the clouds out of my view. I looked through the fog at Lewis and he was facing the same obstacle. Lewis waved me over and Will and Fred came over also. We huddled together and took a break. I ate one of my Baby Ruths. The wet was starting to penetrate my woolen pants and underwear. The temperature was dropping either from the weather, the higher elevation, or both.

We decided to skirt along the base of the cliffs to my side, looking for a passage upward. In about four hundred yards, a small rock chute opened into the cliffs. It was steep and only ten feet wide. Lewis went up first and disappeared into the clouds above.

He yelled down through the fog, "It opens up, above here. I will holler down when I'm all the way up. Then one at a time, you climb up. I will wait up there."

Will went up, then Fred went up, and then I went up. All the time, I was thinking, *Don't they know we have to come back down sometime?*

Baby Ruth

After getting through the chute, the rock slides ended. The mountain gave up its ruggedness and flattened somewhat. Small sapling trees and brush were intermingled with outcrops of rock. We now could travel in single file zigzagging our way up and across the incline in the spitting snow in the clouds.

Time went by and the mountain seemed to flatten more. We finally reached the plateau. It was not flat by any means, but it was not nearly as steep as the face of the mountain. The snow was deeper and came over the top of my boots to my knees. Walking was difficult. We made ourselves comfortable in the snow and ate our lunches. It was now approaching two o'clock. In the late fall, it gets dark early. Lewis and Will decided we would spread out about fifty yards apart and move slowly up into the plateau being on the alert for the elk. We were in the clouds and it was foggy. We could see about twenty-five yards. It was eerily silent. Once again, I was on the far left side. I did not like being so separated and out of sight, but this was not the crowd, the time, or the place to speak my mind.

In what seemed like an eternity, two shots rang out way off to my right. I heard the muffled voice of Fred yell, "They are coming your way!"

My heart raced. I pulled off my trigger glove and placed it in my coat pocket. I pushed back my stocking hat so I could see better. I cocked the hammer of my Winchester 30-30. I started forward, and in less than ten steps, it happened. Uphill to the front of me and slightly to my left in the fog, the shrubs and saplings exploded with motion. Several elk were on a full run. I was so amazed and excited for an instant I forgot I was hunting. I immediately gathered myself and, through wavering sights, fired two shots at the leader. I missed, but the elk leader turned and circled back toward Lewis. The group followed. I ran in the snow uphill as I heard Lewis shoot. Shortly thereafter, the elk reappeared straight ahead and above me. They were no more than forty yards away. As if on command, they stopped. In unison, they tipped their heads back and put their noses high into the air. Their nostrils flared sucking in air as they sniffed the winds. Their ears twitched, front to back and side to side, listening for any hint of a sound in the fog and snow.

I nervously fumbled and removed my other glove so I could firmly grasp my Winchester. I was excitedly in a panic. The elk had not seen me or knew I was near. I was breathing hard and was unsteady on my feet. As best I could, I leveled my sights and emptied my gun at the large cow elk leading the pack. All seven of my shots missed. I saw the snow kick up around the elk as I fired. I softly curse under my breath and said to myself, "You really are a lousy hunter!"

The elk dropped her head down, turned toward me, and looked straight into my eyes. Fumbling with wet cold fingers I shoved two shells in my rifle. The lead elk threw her head into the air and let out a shrill low whistle and bolted straight away from me into the fog. I had not noticed, but below me and to my left was a younger smaller cow elk. She was looking up the hill in the direction of the whistle. She made a quarter turn and set her hind quarters to bolt up the hill as I pointed my gun in her direction. I did not use my sights. I simply pointed the gun as I looked at her head with both eyes open. I fired.

The elk froze in her tracks. Her whole body shivered, and she shuddered and went stiff. For an instant she hung in space, then slowly she tipped over on her side and slide down the mountain in the snow. Her feet pointed upward in the air.

I was completely soaked on the inside of my clothes. I had run over fifty yards in nearly waste deep snow. My trousers were soaked. My stocking hat was down nearly overly my eyes. I was huffing, puffing, and sweating. I realized I had fumbled most of my cartridges into the snow. For some reason, I was very fidgety and nervous. I sat down in the snow to reassemble my outfit, straighten out my shells, get my gloves, and calm myself.

I looked up to see Lewis trudging toward me through the snow. He said, "How many did you get?"

Breathing heavily, I looked up but did not answer.

He continued, "I got a small cow! One shot right through the head! After I shot, they turned back toward you!" He reiterated, "How many did you get?"

I replied, "I think I got one. Maybe a three-year-old cow."

Elk

JERRY HANSON

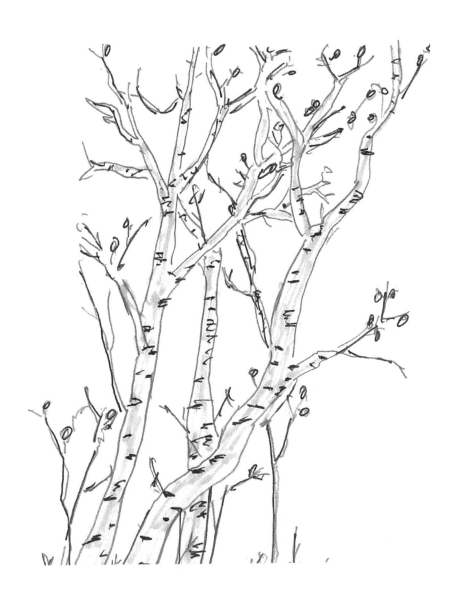

Aspen Trees

He said, "One? Man, you shot about ten times."

I replied, "Yeah, they were running and I could hardly see them."

He said, "Where is the one you shot?"

I said, "She slide down the hill. I hope she stopped! I gotta go see."

Lewis said; "Okay, you do that. I will go get Will and Fred. We will dress out my elk and pull her over to where you are. Okay?"

I dejectedly said, "Yeah okay."

Lewis then said, "Settle down now. We have a lot to do before it turns dark. You did good! This is your first elk. Don't forget to get her bugling teeth!"

He left and I got up and headed over to where my elk had fallen. I followed her skid marks in the snow down the side of the Eagle Peaks. She slid nearly seventy yards in the snow through brush and rock outcroppings. Thank God for a thicket of aspen trees. They stopped her slide or she would have gone over the cliffs.

Upon reaching her carcass, I was anxious to see if I had made a good shot and hoped I had not ruined much of the meat. My shot had struck her high in the neck, seven inches behind her head. Her spine had been completely severed. She had died instantly. There had been no suffering. Death was sudden and no meat was ruined.

I struggled moving her out of the thicket, so I could dress her carcass. I was not especially skilled as a woodsman or a butcher. But, without an audience to critique me, I proceeded forward. I had watched Pa field dress animals. When finished, I concluded I had done a good job. I began to think, *How in the hell are we going to get the elk off this mountain? Dark was fast approaching and we have cliffs and rocks to navigate!*

Lewis, Will, and Fred appeared. All three were pulling on a rope with a yearling elk following behind in the heavy snow. We decided each of us could carry or slide a quarter of the small elk off the mountain today. Will was packing a small collapsible meat saw which we used to carve the elk into quarters.

I said, "Hey, if we leave my elk here tonight the wolves will get her."

Will said, "The wolves aren't up here."

Lewis said, "We'll quarter her up and hide her out on the cliffs in the rocks and cover her in snow. If they are up here, I doubt they can find her in the rocks or in the snow."

We quartered my elk, moved the quarters onto the rock cliffs, and covered them in snow. We pushed the innards and head down the rock slide chute which we were about to ascend. It had now begun to snow heavy with large white fluffy flakes. It was nearly dark.

Down the mountain we went. Will in the lead and this time Lewis was in the rear. Each of us carefully carrying or sliding in the snow with sixty pounds of elk meat, we ascended the Eagle Peaks. We each secured our quarter with rope in case it got away from us and slide down the mountain. Fred said, "It ain't too smart to be tied to an elk on this mountain. We could all end up at the bottom of the mountain!"

Will said, "Be careful!"

About half way down the rock slide, we passed my elks innards. Her head was lodged in the crotch of a small aspen tree. I stopped and untied myself from my elk quarter.

Lewis said, "What are you doing?"

I responded, "I forgot to get her teeth," as I trudged over to her head.

Lewis said, "Hell, hurry up! We'll lose sight of Fred and Will."

Then he yelled, "Hey, you guys, wait a minute. We got to get her teeth."

I cut the bugling teeth from the back of her jaw and carefully placed them deep in my front pockets. It was now dark, still snowing, and getting colder. The wolf pack leader gave out a low mournful and long howl. We all stopped and listened. The howl was not far away, and it seemed to be in front of us. My confidence was lifted knowing we were together and had our weapons. I felt my Winchester and made sure my magazine was loaded.

It was scary crossing the West Branch of Lion Creek in the dark. Snow hung over the banks and covered sheets of thin ice on the slower-moving waters. Will stepped into a hole. The water came up

Elk Bugling Teeth

*(Elk teeth are prized. They are the back molar teeth used to
strip sampling tree leaves. They are not used for bugling!)*

to his waste, and he struggled to keep his balance and hold the elk on his shoulders. Fred quickly steadied him and his load. Together we all helped him get back on safe footing in the shallower water. Traversing through the downed timber was even more difficult. Often we had to stop and lift our elk over downed trees and then crawl over ourselves. It was slow going. The moon was faintly visible in the sky, but the standing trees obscured it most of the time. I was so cold I was shivering. As we exhaled, we could see our breath. We navigated the downed timber section and came into the clear-cut opening. The moon was visible now. We could see the Jeep across the clear cut.

Lewis said, "Stop here for a minute. I need to properly tag this elk."

He completed the task just as another mournful wolf howl pierced the night. This howl was much closer and off to our right. We immediately headed across the clear cut to the Jeep. Will started the jeep and turned the heater to high. We loaded the elk on the top of the jeep and secured it. Nearing midnight we headed out of the Lion Creek drainage in the Eagle Range for the Walker ranch.

Arriving at the Walker ranch, we were surprised to see so many lights in front of the house. A group of rancher pickups were idling with their lights on. A deputy sheriff's Ford Bronco and Game Warden Faust's jeep were in the mix. They were in the process of forming a search party to start looking for us.

Game Warden Earl Faust was a retired Baltimore cop. He moved out west with a big government retirement settlement. Word had circulated to the valley that his settlement was based on fraud, but the Baltimore Police Department wanted to be rid of him. He made sure his wealth was known to the poorer folks in Eagle Valley. Faust never fit into the western way of life and the ranchers and locals avoided him. He had his police band radio in his vehicle, but he also installed a CB radio and spent much of his time listening in on conversations. It always amazed everyone how Faust seemed to show up whenever something in the community was ongoing. He always appeared when there was a problem. He never helped out much but always had his nose

Wolf at Bay

in the affair offering his unwanted opinions or advice. The state game warden had purposefully assigned Faust to the remote Eagle Valley. None of the other wardens wanted to work with or around Faust.

Warden Faust came over by the jeep and quizzed us about our elk. He inspected Lewis's tags. He asked if the elk was a cow and we told him yes. In discussion we also reported we had another cow elk we had to leave on the mountain.

We left half of Lewis's elk with Will for the Walker's use and put our half in Pa's pickup. It was well past midnight. With Pa driving, we started our seventy-mile trek home. I remember Pa querying Lewis, "Why did you guys go up that mountain? The elk was not that important."

Lewis responded, "Pa, we haven't gotten an elk this season. There is only a couple weeks left to get an elk."

Pa said, "I wish you guys had kept quiet about the other elk. It may blizzard tomorrow, and since Faust knows about it, we have to go back and get it."

That was all I remember of the ride home. I fell sound asleep and did not awaken until Ma came to greet us at the pickup.

Pa said, "You boys go on to bed. I will take care of the elk."

Pa had told Uncle Wally we would be back at the ranch in the morning. It was seven thirty, and I felt like I had just gone to bed. We were all up and looking for dry hunting clothes to wear. Ma made a heavy breakfast of oatmeal, toast, ham, and pancakes. We gobbled down our food, grabbed the lunches Ma had made, and headed out the door to Pa's pickup. We got to the Walker ranch at ten fifteen. Wally and Will had loaded their pack horses into the horse trailer and hooked it to their pickup. They were ready to roll.

Wally said, "I know about where you boys came down Eagle Peaks. We can walk the horses around the downed timbers to the west side of the West Branch of Lion Creek. Then we can walk the horses up an old skidding trail I know along the West Branch of Lion Creek. At least the horses can pack the elk from there. That will save

Game Warden Patches

us well over a tough going mile. Will had indicated the second elk was much bigger."

Wally continued, "It is possible to get to that plateau with horses, but it is over a ten-mile hike and the trails are snowed shut. You boys are going to have to climb back up and bring down the elk, like before. That is, if you can find her."

We left Pa and Wally on the Lion Creek logging road as we headed out. They were unloading the horses to outfit them and bring them around the clear-cut and downed timber to the West Branch of Lion Creek.

For three and one-half hours, we struggled our way back up Eagle Peaks. It was even more treacherous hiking in the new snow. Since we knew where to find the chute we had climbed through the day before, our route was more direct. The chute was even more dangerous to navigate. Lewis went up first and got through. He dislodged a small avalanche of snow which crashed down on us and almost caught Will and took him off the mountain.

It was scary and treacherous, but we all got through the chute. Once on the plateau, we tried to orient ourselves and retrace where we had encountered the elk herd. Lewis was the best at that, and soon he found the tree where he had dressed his animal. From there he traced us over to where he met me. Then I lead us to where my elk had become stuck in the aspen thicket. Carefully and methodically in the snow, we began to search and find a quarter of my elk at a time. While we were getting my elk a piece at a time, Lewis scouted around the cliffs for a better place to ascend due to all the new snow. The route we had previously gone down was covered in nearly a foot of fresh snow. We were concerned about an avalanche taking us down the mountain. Lewis found a more gentle exit off the mountain with some benched areas along the way for regrouping. The problem was we had to haul my elk about one hundred yards up the mountain before crossing over to our new route.

My elk was at least twice as big as Lewis's animal had been. Working in pairs, we got the elk up the hill. Lewis and I were sitting on our last elk quarter as Will and Fred were bringing in their last

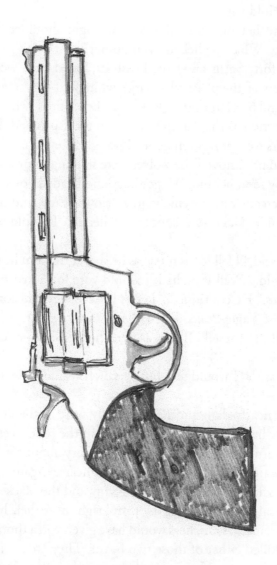

357 Revolver

piece. Lewis quietly removed his 357 magnum pistol from its holster and said, "Hold still!"

At head height, he fired across my right shoulder. As my ears rang, I said, "What the hell are you doing?"

Then forty yards away the brush exploded with wolves. There were a dozen of them led by a large white and gray male followed shortly behind by a large pure black male. Lewis fired two more rounds in their direction as they disappeared into the aspen and shrubs.

My ears were still ringing, but I was glad Lewis had spooked the wolves. I did not know if the wolves were stalking us or waiting to see if we left any food behind. We got busy and headed down the mountain. The descent was extremely quiet, slow, steady, and uneventful.

Will said, "Next time, shoot a smaller elk. This old babe weighs a ton."

Lewis said, "Hell for as much as he shot, I thought he got six elk."

Will said, "Well if he had, I would vote for donating the other to the wolves." He continued, "I can't believe they had come clear up on top of the Eagle Peaks. My dad says our cattle are a hell of a lot easier to kill than an elk. If he was here, he would shoot every one of those wolves."

Lewis said, "I would too, but Pa says it would cause trouble that we don't need."

It was nearly dark and Pa and Wally were at the creek waiting for us. They had made a small camp site in the pine trees and had a camp fire burning. We excitedly told our story about finding the elk in the snow and that the wolves had been near us again.

Wally said, "Did you see the big gray and the black one?"

Lewis said, "Yeah, I shot my pistol right over their heads."

Wally said, "Us ranchers would have given you a thousand bucks if you had killed either of those two beasts. They are cattle killers."

Just at that time from out of the woods, Game Warden Faust silently rode his horse into camp. He had been secretively lurking nearby in the trees.

He said, "Wally, I heard you! You know those wolves are protected. If I hear of any of you shooting or shooting at one of those wolves, I will ticket you and see to it you get fined!"

Then he turned and looked at Lewis and said, "So, young man, did I hear you say you shot at the wolves?"

Pa jumped in and said, "Faust, you heard no such thing. There are six people here that can attest to that. He said he fired into the air. That was our agreed-upon signal for when they would start down the mountain and nothing more."

Faust retorted, "I was talking to the boy."

Pa said, "Look, Faust, he is my boy and he is a minor. You can talk to me. If you didn't always hide behind that badge, we could settle this like men."

Faust said, "Are you threatening an officer of the law?"

Wally stepped in and said, "Look, Faust, I don't think any of us six heard a threat. You know you snuck in here on us in the quiet of the snow. We did not see you coming. As usual, you show up uninvited, and instead of helping, you cause trouble. We all live out here, scratch out a living, help each other out, and try to be good neighbors. To you this is just a big game! By the way, Faust, you are supposed to wear red or orange on your uniform during hunting season. Why aren't you?"

Faust ignored Wally, glared at us, and said, "I will be waiting at the animal check station I had set up on the highway today. You better be coming through it before nightfall with that animal."

Faust turned his horse and rode off into the dark.

I was startled when Ma said, "You better get a move on'. The Wertzs will be waiting for your help. Those girls don't know how to milk cows! I told Marilyn you would be there before five."

"Wild animals...have been placed in your power to be used for food..." (Genesis 9:3).

"Do not neglect to do good and share what you have..." (Hebrews 13:16).

Jerry Hanson. 2019

FAME

As years passed, things changed. At least Jonathan's perspective of things changed. Every day of the school year, Jonathan walked to and from school on a country road. There was nothing special about the country road, but to Jonathan it was special. It was just over a mile from Jonathan's house to Day Creek School. There must be no less than three million rocks in that one-mile stretch of road. Some rocks were no bigger than a grain of sand, and other rocks stuck out of the ground just far enough to let you know they were bigger than you. No one would ever know exactly how many rocks were in that road, and why should they? The number of rocks in that road was simply not important. They were just rocks. Jonathan walked this windy mile, in dust, mud, and snow in both directions for eight years. Other than kicking and counting rocks, Jonathan did not learn much on those treks. More often than not, he lost count of the rocks as his young mind meandered off in various directions much like the lanes of the road. Sometimes Jonathan's mind mulled over things that happened that day at school. Sometimes he thought about what he would do when he got home. But mostly, Jonathan dreamed of grandeur and fame. His dreams were exciting and eliminated all his worries and troubles. Heading home from school was Jonathan's own precious time, and he loved those good old days.

Jack Clark was eight years older than Jonathan. Jack lived in a two-bedroom rundown house off a muddy lane connected to Day Creek Road. Jack was scrappy and athletic. But most importantly

Country Road

Jack was a good enough natural athlete to start as quarterback on the Benton High School football team. Day Creek School was twenty-one miles from the town of Benton and the high school. With side trips and numerous stops, it took two and one-half hours for the high school bus to deliver Jack to school. That fact meant Jack or any other kid from Day Creek could not practice after school with the football team and accordingly could not play football for the Benton Bulls. Edna Allison was the head bookkeeper for the largest granary in Benton. Edna purposefully worked late every night so Jack could play football for the Benton Bulls. Edna waited and picked Jack up after football practice and delivered him home every night during the season.

Edna was a hero in Day Creek for her chauffeuring of Jack, and Jack was a hero for being the quarterback of the Benton Bulls. Jack put the folks on Day Creek Road on the Benton County map of importance. The important stock rose even higher when the Bulls won the state championship and Jack was named first team all-state. Jack's parents held a community party on their muddy lane with real factory bottled beer, bottled soda, hamburgers, and hot dogs. Everybody that lived on Day Creek Road, except the Tafts and Bud Phelps, came to the Clark's party. Jonathan's father was proud of Jack and told him so several times. Jonathan was impressed with Jack. Jack was strong and athletic. To Jonathan, he was also a genuine and sincere person.

Slowly shuffling toward home and counting rocks in the dusty heat, Jonathan imagined playing quarterback for the Benton Bulls, just like Jack. Maybe someday he thought, it just could happen. After all Jack came from Day Creek and lived on Day Creek Road just like Jonathan. Jonathan forgot about his homework assigned for the next day. He did not care that he had no ideas for his 4-H presentation coming due. He blocked it all out. He was getting the job done as the Bulls quarterback between kicking and counting rocks.

Fall came and on a hot dusty afternoon the freshman class showed up at Benton Memorial Field to begin football practice.

"Line up, you knuckleheads!" yelled Coach Mack. He continued, "Get in there and get your gear! Be back here in ten minutes! Hurry up!"

Simultaneously, forty six freshmen tried to squeeze through a single leaf doorway, that is, all except the dozen country kids not used to the city way of "get in there or get left behind." Freshman uniforms and equipment consist of what is left from the varsity and junior varsity teams. They are composed of odd sizes, mismatched pairs, torn and broken pads, and faded or shrunken shirts. Jonathan's pads were far too large. His pants were too big and his kneepads hung below his knees. Jonathan mentally decided to become a man at that very moment and hereto forward would be known as Jon.

With his new name, his new bravado, and his speak up voice, Jon yelled at the equipment manager, "Hey, Slim, give me a different pair of pants and some other shoulder pads!"

Slim slammed the door in Jon's face as he mumbled, "You're lucky you got that!"

Jon along with the stragglers pulled on their misfit uniforms and finally headed out the door to practice. They were met with Coach Mack's shouting, "You look like a bunch of slobs! Don't show up late again for my practice! Give me twenty pushups, right now!" Coach Mack screamed, "Line up for calisthenics, now! I mean right now!"

Jon thought to himself, *What the heck's all this yelling and screaming about? Did Jack have to put up with this stuff too? Is this what makes good football players?*

Jon decided if Jack had to do this, he could too.

Scrimmage time came.

Coach Mack yelled, "Give me last years starting team from junior high." Out ran eleven players in much better looking and fitting uniforms than Jon's.

Then Assistant Coach Cloud yelled, "Give me the second team from junior high." Out ran eleven more, better dressed and equipped players.

Then a senior coach's helper said, "Who has played quarterback?" Jon slowly raised his hand. He was ignored.

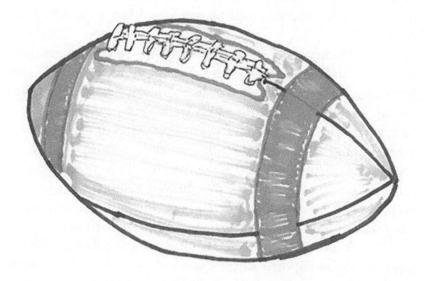

High School Football

Once again, the helper stated louder, "Who else plays quarterback?"

Some kids answered, "Hey, Tim, you played some quarterback at Saint Josephs."

Jon raised his hand even higher and said, "I play quarterback."

The helper ignored Jon again and said, "Tim get out here."

The senior helper coach formed one more offensive team of eleven players. Then a junior helper told the remaining players to make up a final squad. Jon grabbed the quarterback spot and the other disheveled and confused players joined him to make up the last squad.

Over the next eight weeks, the players were given a playbook of formations and signals that the varsity team used under Coach Kapp. Jon studied the playbook to the demise of his Math and English lessons. Jon cajoled and tutored his teammates to master the very basic plays, who to block, how to pass block, and to talk with each other. In practice sessions, the first two squads worked out against the starting defensive squad. Late in the practice, Jon's squad got to run a few plays against the defensive unit. With little fanfare, Jon and his group kept a positive attitude, had fun, and improved each week. They were of little notice to Coach Mack and his assistants.

The Benton High freshmen football team usually holds scrimmage games among themselves. There are no other nearby schools that have freshman teams. Benton is by far the largest high school in the county and other county schools are so small they play six-man football. Due to expense, the freshman team does not travel. However, Moore County brings all their teams to Benton for yearly rivalry games. That year Benton's varsity team lost badly, the junior varsity also lost badly, but the freshman squad was ahead by seven points at half time. Head Varsity Coach Kapp appeared on the sidelines and told Coach Mack and Coach Cloud he wanted to see all the freshman squads play. Coach Kapp said, "I know you want to win this game, but I want to see any potential talent in this class."

The first team had played the first half of the game. The second squad started the second half and was scheduled to play all of the third quarter. They struggled and eventually fell behind 21 to 14. Tim and the third squad started the fourth quarter. In three series they lost yardage, fumbled the ball twice, and threw an interception. They were unorganized, confused, and started picking on one another for their shortcomings. The only thing saving the game from getting out of control was the first-string defense. With five minutes remaining in the game, Jon and his squad entered the game. Still trailing 21 to 14, they got the ball on Moore County's twenty-yard line.

Jon was anxious and his team was noticeably nervous. The grandstands were full and the coaches were watching intently. In the huddle, Jon calmed his team by telling them, "We are going to run simple straightforward plays, nothing complicated. Don't worry! Stick to doing your job just like we practice, talk to each other, and help each other out."

Calling only very simple and basic plays, Jon's team methodically marched down the field, gaining three and four yards with each play. He told the lineman and running backs to carefully listen for his signal to either run a play to the right or the left. Jon watched where the opposing center, defensive lineman, and middle-line backers positioned themselves. He called a color for the right side or a number for left side. It was simple and it was working.

They reached their own twenty-five-yard line, and Moore County ran in a fresh defensive unit. This unit wore newer and fancier uniforms. They were bigger, faster, and better organized. It was Moore County's junior varsity squad! Coach Mack and Coach Cloud began pacing the sidelines and yelling plays at Jon. Coach Kapp keenly watched the action from the sidelines. Against this new defense, Jon called a right off tackle play. The halfback barely got the ball back to the line of scrimmage. This defense was tougher and better. The next play, Jon called off left tackle and they lost a yard. They were losing yards and going backward!

Coach Mack and Coach Cloud simultaneously were yelling, "Jon, it's third down, run outside! Run outside! Jon, run the 994 outside! Call the sweep! Call the sweep! 994!"

Jon heard their pleas but ignored their demands. The sweep plays they wanted had been only practiced by the first team. Jon knew the plays his squad handled best. In the huddle Jon called a

Football Stadium

347-option run play. He told Burt, a halfback, "I will fake a handoff to you. You must help fake the handoff too! Draw their tackles and linebackers into the line, like you have the ball! We must sell the handoff and you must sell the run!"

Jon told the left end, Trey, "Go out slower for seven yards, fake left, and cut right. Make the cut hard and sharp. Then run as fast across the field as you can. Make a commotion, yell for the ball, wave your hands, and act like you are receiving a pass. Sell this play to the defense!"

Jon told the slot back, Chris, "Follow Trey out, and when he cuts slant right and deep across the field as fast as you can run. I won't have much time, so be ready. I am looking to pass to you!"

Jon smiled and to lessen the tension said, "Chris, don't forget to catch the ball!"

Chris smiled back and said, "Yeah, right!"

Jon told the left guard Larry, "Pull to the right and stay in front of me as I roll to the right. Block for me. If our guys can't get open, I will have to run the ball around the end."

Larry replied, "Got it!"

Jon told everyone, "This is it, guys! This is our big play! Do your jobs! It will work!"

They clapped hands in unison and broke the huddle. Immediately after the set formation, the center hiked the ball. Moore County was not fully ready for the quick snap and was caught off guard. Their defensive backs came up to defend Trey. Their linebackers and lineman collapsed on Burt, who did not have the ball. Larry blocked in front of Jon. Jon purposefully threw the ball over Treys stretched out hands. Speeding across and down the field, the ball landed perfectly in Chris's arms. Chris scored! Sammy came into the game and made the extra point. The game was tied again!

With one minute and forty seconds remaining in the game, Jon and his squad happily scampered off the field. As the ball was being prepared to kick to Moore County, Coach Kapp said, "Nice job, boys!" to Jon and his team.

As Jon stood on the sidelines watching the kickoff, Coach Mack slapped him on the helmet and said, "That was not the play I yelled at you to run, Jon!"

Football Game

From under his helmet, Jon could see coach was frowning. He said, "Sorry, coach. With all the noise out there, I could not hear."

Coaches Mack and Cloud in unison replied, "Yeah, right!"

Jon looked up as the ball was being kicked off. Moore County's JV team returned the kickoff for a touchdown. Jon adjusted and pulled his helmet on, and snapped the straps into place. He said to his squad, "Get ready to go. We won't have much time to try and score."

As they headed onto the field, Coach Mack and Coach Cloud were yelling for Bruce and the first squad to get on the field. Jon and his team were called back to the bench.

Bruce and the first team did not realize they were now playing against the Moore County JV defense. On the first play, Moore County overpowered the line. Bruce was sacked for a seven-yard loss. With less than forty seconds left in the game, Bruce's team jumped off sides. They were penalized five yards. The next play Bruce dropped back to pass and was quickly thrown to the ground for a ten-yard loss. As Bruce went down, he fumbled the ball.

Moore recovered the fumble and ran out the clock. Moore County won the game 28 to 21. Once again, Moore County had swept the Benton Bulls.

Dejected and disappointed, Jon slowly trudged out of the stadium. Coach Kapp appeared beside him. Coach Kapp said, "Jon, you did a great job in there. I am impressed how well you manage your team. I know you don't have the biggest or best players but keep up the good work. Stay positive. It will pay off!" Coach Kapp slapped Jon on the shoulder pads and said, "Good job!"

Jon went to bed happy that night. He looked at the ceiling in his room for a long time. He knew his rag tag team had done well. He fell asleep with a smile on his face. At Monday's practice, Jon was moved to second team quarterback, but none of his squad was moved up. When Jon went into the huddle with his new team, he was uncomfortable. Jon was not part of the junior high crowd. They considered him an unproven country kid. The team lacked focus. They picked on each other. They were competitive and jealous of one another. They spent their time protecting their social clique. Self-glorification, self-interest, and personal attention were their cravings. They thought such would advance them individually to first team. They would not listen to Jon's play calling or follow his lead. During practice, Jon would call a play in the huddle to the retort of two or three other players saying, "No! That play won't work! Let's run that pass play from last week." Or they would make up some exotic double handoff play. The team was unorganized, undisciplined, and off-sides far too often on signal calls. It was no fun for Jon, but the season was coming to an end. Jon hung around his old team whenever he could. They were not fast, or big, or cool. They were just solid players who tried to work as a team. Jon missed his old team.

The season ended and Benton High held their yearly assembly. The football program was honored. The freshmen were awarded the blue and gold freshman football insignias. Coach Kapp announced he was accepting the head football coaching job at his alma mater, the Redmond Raiders. Kapp said, "I am quite sure when this freshman class become seniors, the Raiders football team will have their hands full."

Jon wished Coach Kapp would have stayed at Benton High.

Jon was slowly becoming aware that Benton County sports was the only venue in the valley for citizens to attach too. High school football was king, and with the six-month long winter, basketball came close behind. Baseball was played outside of high school in the American Legion program. Nationally, baseball was very popular, but in Benton, it was a distant third in popularity. Jon and his brother Jim were the baseball stars of a motley rural team. Jon was a good defensive player, a rather good pitcher, but an exceptional hitter.

Competition to make a Benton football team increased as the grades progressed upward. One day for no reason at all, it dawned on Jon that the genetics of his mother being five feet tall and father being five feet and eight inches tall, most likely, would lead to him not being a large guy. Jon took refuge in the victim role and blamed his lack of size on some of his football setbacks.

Jon soon realized politics played a far larger role in Benton sports than size. Bruce, the first team quarterback, was from junior high. Bruce's father owned a business in Benton, was on the Benton

Bench, and handled all the insurance for the schools. The fullback's father was a Benton alumnus, a college hero from the U, and had attended school with the new head coach.

Jon also became aware that the coaches liked to survey your family's sports history as well as your parents' size as they decided who got what playing positions. Every parent as well as every kid wanted to be the star on the Benton varsity football team. Only a handful would ever achieve such. Positions that garnered media attention were sought after. Starting positions of quarterback, half-back, fullback, part of the defensive unit, or an end were valued. Lineman never made the news, the newspaper, or were honored out for great games.

Jon's father did not encourage him to play football or any other sport. His father, without directly saying so, implied football was a waste of time. Getting a job would be of far more value. However, he did tell Jon, "If you are going to play, work hard, keep a positive attitude, and do a good job."

Jon was on his own at Benton High. His mother was well aware of the social importance of high school notoriety, but she was of little help in navigating the politics and interactions of the Benton football program or the Benton Bench. Many individual players were simply never given a chance to play various positions. The coaches had to please the Benton Bench, but they also wanted to deliver stars to local university programs. It gave them status and the possibility of moving up in the coaching ranks. The only thing that seemed to overcome the politics at Benton High was if the coach put together teams that won, preferably winning the state championship or at least being in the state championship game.

Jon was just as good as Bruce at playing quarterback. Bruce was an inch taller than Jon, but they weighed the same. Jon was faster and in general a better leader. However, Bruce was part of the junior high crowd; his father was a Benton businessman and an officer of the Benton Bench. The new coaches immediately bought into the politics of the school and town.

Fall arrived. Try outs for varsity and junior varsity football began. Only sixty players would be selected, and it was announced that two freshmen would be moved up to the varsity squad. The freshman's parents both had played football at the U or state. Jon was assigned the second team quarterback job behind Bruce. Jon soon realized his role was to run the offensives of upcoming opponents against the varsity defense in full contact scrimmages. Coach Mack was Jon's direct coach. Mack would call all the plays Jon was to run. Jon could look over the center and see several plays that would rip through the defense. He could not run those plays. Mack insisted the other teams would run the plays he was calling. Jon knew a quarterback or coach of any value would begin to call the same plays he was seeing. On one set of plays, Jon told the center to hick the ball and block straight forward if he pushed on the center. Jon pushed, the center hiked the ball, and Jon ran straight through the defense for a touchdown. Coach Mack slapped Jon on the head and said, "Jon, that was not the play you were to run!"

Jon came to dislike Coach Mack. In full scrimmages, Jon was continually tackled hard and roughed up. One late afternoon practice, Jon was gang tackled by several defensive players. He fell awkwardly on his wrist. The bone in his wrist was cracked. Jon wore a cast, was out for the season, but had to attend practices. After his broken arm incident, Coach Mack was directed to stop "full contact until the end of the scrimmage play." Although playing in only three games, Jon was awarded a varsity football letter at the yearly assembly.

Fall arrived and football season came again. The Benton Bulls had new coaches. Max Reynolds was head coach and his buddy, Bob Baker, was head assistant coach. Coach Mack remained the offensive coach. When the season started before any tryouts, Jon was once again assigned second string quarterback behind Bruce. Jon was back in his old job running the upcoming opponent plays against the first-string varsity. Once in a while, when Bruce took a break, Jon ran the first-string offense at quarterback. Jon felt he was far short of Jack Clark's football accomplishments at Benton High. After two weeks, Jon told Coaches Baker and Mack he did not want to play quarterback any longer.

Both coaches were put out and mad. Coach Baker snapped at Jon, "Suit yourself, Jon. I doubt you will get to play at any other position!"

Jon joined the halfback pool and became one of a half dozen sideline halfbacks who rarely played. The team struggled. Head Coach Reynolds's offensive scheme focused on outside running or sweep passing. It placed a premium on downfield blocking. His scheme did not focus on power blocking at the line but on speed to get outside and downfield. The coaches were extremely frustrated with lack of downfield blocking and in practice continually focused and practiced outside blocking plays. To be successful at downfield blocking, you must be aware of how the play is setting up, where the defensive players are coming from, where your fellow offensive players are located, and have speed and balance to maintain your position. Speed gets the blocker out in front of the play. Awareness gets the blocker into the right position, and balance keeps the blocker from simply being pushed out of the way by a defensive player.

In one grueling practice session, a starting halfback lost his shoe. Jon was standing on the sidelines near a frustrated Coach Reynolds. Reynolds pushed Jon forward and said, "Get in there! Let's go again!"

Coach Baker recalled the previous play and Jon sprinted to the outside, hesitated for the ball carrier to close, and as the defense collapsed on the runner, Jon wiped three of them out with a cross body block. It was not hard for Jon. The defensive players were watching the ball carrier and not Jon. Jon simply wiped them out. The play went for a touchdown.

Coach Reynolds screamed, "Yes! Yes! That is how it is supposed to work!"

He said, "Who threw that block?"

Coach Mack responded unenthusiastically, "That was Jon."

Immediately, Jon was converted to a pulling guard position in the starting offensive line. Jon thought, *What the heck? I was in the halfback slot! Why am I going into the line as a guard?*

Jon's Day Creek daydreams of Jack and being quarterback surfaced again. He thought, *Darn it! Jack was not only the starting Benton quarterback but was selected first team all-state. Not only am I not the*

Offensive Lineman

quarterback, I am not even a halfback. I am a down lineman! I have worked hard! I have kept a good attitude! And I think I have done a good job! This is just not working out for me. Jon kept his disappointment to himself and kept trying his best at practice.

Jon swallowed his pride. He did want to help the team, but mostly he wanted another varsity letter for his letter sweater. Jack had three stripes, and so far, so did Jon. Jon played right and left guard. He was five feet and ten inches tall and weighted a trim muscular 175 pounds. Jon played against guys as big as 220 pounds. He was quicker, faster, just as tough, and smarter than most of them. Benton finished the season 8-3. Coach Reynolds and Coach Baker called it a building year with a new system. Benton Bench and the community accepted the explanation and waited for the next football season.

Football started up again and Jon was slotted as starting senior pulling guard. Jon started but shared plays with Stan Bailey and Ralph Staves. Plays were sent into the game through the guards. Stan's father was an assistant football coach, the head track coach, and taught at Benton High. Ralph's father was on Benton Bench and had a business in town. Jon was quicker, more astute, and simply better than both Stan and Ralph. Jon played most plays. Benton finished the season 11-0-1. Benton's varsity was praised as one of the great sports teams from Benton High. Although Benton had tied Moore County Marauders earlier in the year, they fell to them 13 to 7 in the state championship game.

Thirty three players were selected for all-state honors, and Jon was one of those players. Jon was selected as second team all-state guard. To Jon, guard was not a glorious position, especially for someone who wanted to play quarterback. At the time, he thought the honor insignificant. Benton got seven all-state players and Moore County got nine. Of the Benton seven all-state players selected, only one of them in Jon's opinion was politically connected. Jon knew the other six players were the best players.

That spring Jon once again felt slighted. His all-state football teammates, plus a few other players, were receiving scholarship offers to play football at universities and colleges. Jon was getting no offers.

Coach Baker approached Jon in the hall one day at school and said, "Jon, are you interested in playing college football?"

Jon responded, "No one seems very interested in me, coach."

Baker replied, "I went to Mount Ridge College, and I can get you a scholarship to play football there if you are interested. You gotta let me know right away."

Mount Ridge College offered none of the curriculums Jon was interested in. Besides, Jon had better chances at baseball scholarships at larger schools.

Jon told Coach Baker, "Coach, thank you for thinking of me, but I am going to go to state and study veterinary."

Baker responded, "Okay, that is probably a good choice for you. You know you are probably too small to play in a college line."

Baker's response hurt Jon's feelings, but deep down, Jon knew he was truthful. Jon's roommate at state was one of the starting offensive guards on the football team. He was six feet and four inches tall and weighed a trim 265 pounds. However, Jon noticed he was the same size as the starting quarterback. Jon focused on veterinarian school and only played intramural sports. He was good and the baseball and football coaches asked him if he would like to try out. Jon declined.

Time fly's by. It has been over thirty years since Jon played football for the Benton Bulls. He was back in Benton for a family visit and was meeting his brother Ron to play a round of golf. As Jon finished lacing his shoes in the club house, Ron said, "Hey, Jon, come over here. I want to introduce you to someone."

Jon finished tying his shoes and walked over to Ron standing near a gray-haired and slightly stooped older gentleman.

Ron said, "Do you know who this is?"

The man was grinning broadly and looking intently at Jon. Jon peered back at him and smiled too. Jon could not place or recognize the stranger. He had no idea who he was.

Politely Jon said, "I'm sorry, but I don't remember you. My memory is not what it used to be."

The stranger broadened his smile even wider, stuck out his hand, and said, "That's okay. My memory is not as good as it used to be either. I am Jack Clark from Day Creek. Do you remember me now?"

Jon chuckled with delight, stuck out his hand, and said, "Oh my goodness, Jack! What an honor to see you! You never knew, but you were and are my hero from Day Creek and Benton High! Oh my, good to see you!" Jon continued to grasp and pump Jack's hand.

Jack smiled and said, "Well, Jon, you are my hero too! We are the only guys ever to play varsity football for the Bulls from Day Creek. That is an accomplishment!"

Jon responded, "Yup, I guess so. But you, Jack! You were not only starting varsity quarterback. You were first team all-state quarterback! That is an all-time accomplishment!"

Jack said, "Well from what I recall, you were all-state in both football and baseball."

Jon said, "Only second team in football. You were first team quarterback, Jack, for the most popular and important sport in Benton County!"

Jack replied, "Well, thanks. In my old age, I find compliments more pleasing than I ever did when I was younger."

Ron interjected, "If you two don't stop gushing over each other and get a move on, we will miss our tee time!"

They all laughed and headed for the tee box on the first hole.

On the fifth hole, Jack asked, "Jon, did you ever think you could go further in a sports career?"

Jon seemed to pause for a long time and did not answer Jack. Jon was remembering all of his daydreams on Day Creek Road. Being a football hero for the Benton Bulls and being an all-state quarterback like Jack flashed through his memory. He thought of how his perspective on life, things, and sports had shifted over the years. On the way to the next tee box, Jon answered Jack.

In response he said, "When I was young, I dreamed of being famous at sports. It was an unrealistic view. I was a daydreamer. When things did not work out, I became disgruntled and disappointed. I blamed genetics, my size, my parents, the coaches, and even Benton County on my lack of fame. Today, and especially after talking with you, I realize my experiences in sports were character building and I

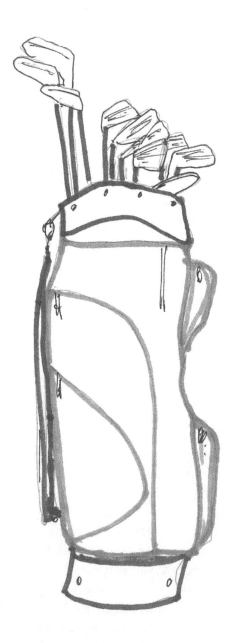

A Round of Golf

am glad I participated. My life has worked out fine, without sports or fame. I have a good family and I consider myself a good veterinarian. I would not have been successful to my satisfaction in sports if I had gone on. Participating in intramural sports programs but focusing on school and a career was the right decision for me. How about you, Jack? Do you wish you had gone on in sports?"

Jack responded, "I got a full-ride scholarship to the U. But I did not care for the effort and work required to play football at that level. I was continually bruised and sore. Football was beating up my body. I realized I was not cutthroat or competitive enough to start or to even get playing time as some of the other guys. I am not critical of them, but I was not like them. I got four years of free schooling and I needed the money. My family didn't have much. I graduated and have worked for the gas company for thirty-three years now. I have a lot of aches and pains in my old age, from football. I told my son to stick to golf!" He chuckled.

The round of golf was finished, and they headed for the club house to enjoy a beer. For Jon, it was more than a fun outing, and he thanked Ron for setting up the round of golf with Jack. He graciously thanked Jack for being such a good hero from Day Creek.

They collected their clubs and started toward their cars in the parking lot. They stopped at Jon's Cadillac convertible as Jon placed his golf clubs in the trunk. Jack said, "Jon, did you ever get to ride in the Fourth of July parade in the mayor's old Cadillac convertible?"

Jon replied, "No, that honor was never mine. I remember Mayor Benson's old gunboat Cadillac, though. I remember when some Benton athlete had gotten famous and returned to town, the mayor would have them ride down Main Street with him in that old Cadillac. They would have the top down and be at the head of the parade! Did you get that honor, Jack?"

Jack said, "Nope, our state championship team got to ride on a flatbed truck in the parade but not with the mayor. Our class never got many honors, except for that one year with our state champion football team. What about your class?"

A Cold Beer

Jon responded, "The only thing I can say about my class is I married the prettiest, smartest, sweetest, and nicest girl in the class. Yup, I could not have daydreamed how that would come about!"

Jack laughed and slapped Jon on the back and departed with Ron toward their cars.

Jon drove from the golf course to pick up his wife at the shopping mall. Once again, he reminisced about his rock-kicking expectations and daydreams on Day Creek Road. He remembered the Day Creek residents and his father being impressed with Jack. He recognized the reality of the Day Creek folks was their being impressed with the fame Jack brought to the community. Jack was a decent normal person who played high school football pretty well. No one on Day Creek Road knew much about Jack these days. Surely, they knew less about Jon these days. Young boys need heroes and good role models. Jack was a good role model. Coach Kapp was a good role model. Dad was a good role model too. Dad had put Jack on a pedestal for doing well, not for being famous. Dad never thought much of football or sports. Dad and Coach Kapp's advice to "work hard, be positive, do a good job" was so true.

Jon pulled into the mall and waited for this wife to come to their meeting place. He continued thinking, *Maybe daydreaming lets your mind work without restrictions. Maybe unrealistic daydreams force a person to eventually deal with and accept reality. Sometimes, unfulfilled dreams might be painful, but they may be a necessary step in becoming a mature adult. As one matures, perspective comes into play.*

Jon's wife opened the Cadillac door, placed some packages behind the seat, and then sat down. They drove out of the mall parking lot and stopped at a red light before entering Main Street. Jon looked at his wife and said, "Did you have a fun shopping outing?"

She replied, "Yes, I did. Did you have a good day?"

Jon responded, "I had a fun time and great day!" He added, "I love you very much."

She smiled and said, "I love you too."

Pushing the automatic retraction buttons on the dash, the top on the Cadillac convertible folded down. When the light changed

Cadillac Convertible

from red to green, Jon turned right and very slowly preceded down Main Street.

> *"Dreaming instead of doing is foolishness…"*
> *(Ecclesiastes 5:7)*

> *"When I was a child, I spoke, acted, and reasoned like a child…as a man I gave up childish ways." (1 Corinthians 13:11)*

Jerry Hanson. 2017

THE POLITICIANS

Gregory came into the world on a miserable wintery day in Connecticut. Gregory's birth required his mother, Grace, to labor over thirty-seven hours. Gregory's father, Grayson, was not present when he entered the world.

Grace had meticulously selected a midwife in anticipation of Gregory's arrival. Grace and her longtime college roommate had studied nursing and adamantly believed in natural home delivery of infants. But after thirty hours of painful labor with little result, the midwife became concerned. She called Grayson to come home from his busy tax preparation job. Together, they bundled up a weak and distraught Grace and traveled the thirty-three miles to the regional hospital. Grace's college friend followed through the chilling rain in Grace's car. She was going to help with the admission paperwork upon arrival at the hospital.

The paperwork for admissions and payments was not going well or quickly. Grace shrieked out in pain in the reception area, and the emergency room physician came STAT. He ordered the nurses to take Grace immediately to the delivery area. Grayson, the midwife, and Grace's friend were left explaining how payment to the hospital and doctors would be assured.

Grace was placed in a labor room she shared with three expectant mothers. Each mother soon departed for delivery, leaving a troubled and frail Grace with her pain. Finally, a delivery doctor told Grace and Grayson that labor needed to be induced for the health

Maternity Hospital

of Grace and the child. Initially, Grace and the midwife objected, both insisting on a completely natural birth. Six more hours passed, and Grayson sought out the doctor to help induce labor. The midwife had departed for home and her family. Grayson signed the papers to allow a drug induced delivery and assured Grace it was for the best. Grayson understood the birth would most likely happen within hours. He needed to go to the office briefly but would return promptly to the hospital. Grayson left for his accounting job.

The doctors dispensed medications to Grace and completed the necessary injections. Within fifteen minutes, Grace was in the delivery room. With the help of forceps, Gregory was delivered before Grayson could return from his office.

Gregory did not come easily or quietly. He kicked, screamed, twisted, and turned. The delivery nurse almost dropped him. The doctors and nurses struggled to perform the usual and rudimentary inspections. Finally, out of frustration and his uncooperativeness, they pronounced Gregory normal. Gregory was not normal.

Grace was given a relaxing agent, some light food, lots of liquids, and promptly fell into an exhaustive sleep. Still kicking and screaming, Gregory was taken to the nursery and turned over to the staff. For more than four hours, he continued his kicking, screaming, tossing, and turning. Due to his disruptive behavior, the nurses moved Gregory in his incubator to a room away from the other newborns. Finally, out of pure exhaustion, he fell asleep.

When Grayson found out Gregory had arrived and Grace was sedated, he stayed at work to finalize some pressing work. He returned to the hospital as the nursing shifts were changing. Grace was still asleep, and Gregory was in his private room, asleep. Grayson went into the nursery and looked down upon a cooing and giggling newborn. The baby smiled and kicked his feet in delight. Grayson was delighted and had never felt so proud.

After a couple of hours, Grace awoke and was sitting up. Grayson went into the nursery and asked for the baby. The nurse wrapped the infant tightly in a warming blanket, and Grayson brought him into Grace. Grace was cuddling the baby, and the baby was cooing and smiling. Another nurse rushed into the room and exclaimed, "You have the Reed baby! Who gave him to you?"

The nurse promptly grabbed the baby from Grace's arms and left the room. Immediately, Grace and Grayson demanded to see Gregory. Two nurses came in and proclaimed, "There are no other babies in the nursery?"

The neonatal floor of the hospital exploded in panic. The nurses and staff begin frantically searching for Gregory. Grace was distraught and had to be sedated again. Grayson was angry, frustrated, and threatened legal action. Finally, a janitor said, "There is a baby, screaming his head off downstairs in room 110."

Out the door flew the nurses with Grayson close behind. Down a flight of stairs they scurried, and sure enough, Gregory was screaming, yelling, kicking, fussing, and mad as a wet hen in his incubator in room 110.

That is how Gregory Graham came into the world. Mad! No, mad as a wet hen! Grace took Gregory and tried to calm him. Gregory pushed her off and kicked his feet. Grace tried to nurse Gregory, and when he was able to attach, he bit down so hard Grace cried out. The nurse took Gregory, and they feed him bottled milk. Gregory ate and burped, ate and burped, kicked and cried, ate and burped, until he fell asleep.

Gregory came home, and much to Grace's dismay, he was not a perfect baby. Gregory constantly and continually cried, fussed, and demanded to be held. When he was held, he screamed to be put down. When he was put down, he screamed to be held. Grace was frustrated.

A few months passed, and it became obvious that Gregory was not fully normal. Gregory had suffered some medical damage within the labor process and the assisted birthing process which the delivery team in their haste had not recognized. Gregory was mentally bright, but his head was oversized and cocked slightly to one side. As Gregory matured, it became obvious his right arm would be stunted and did not have full motion. His spine was misaligned which caused his body to tilt to the left. He dragged his right leg slightly. He had to wear thick glasses to obtain 20/40 vision. Gregory was mentally bright but a functioning bundle of imperfect muscles and bones.

Initially, Grace and Grayson embraced the situation of raising Gregory, but Gregory continued to remain extremely difficult and demanding. He utilized his strong will and intellect to finagle his every demand. Embarrassing Grace by throwing uncontrollable fits in front of Grace's friends was Gregory's specialty. When Gregory became of school age, decisions had to be made for his education. Gregory tested well above average mentally but was ranked socially challenged and, of course, physically deformed. Grace insisted Gregory attend a special private school in a nearby town. The school was very expensive, and Grayson didn't earn the kind of money to afford the school.

Grace decided to enroll Gregory in the local public school system. She promptly demanded that the school district accommodate all Gregory's special needs. Grace decided she would integrate Gregory's social education at home. Grayson reluctantly agreed to the arrangement. Grace became Gregory's advocate and an ever-present nuisance to Gregory's teachers and the school district. After two years, of continual tantrums, demands, and outrageous behavior, Grace's patience and nerves wore thin. She insisted Grayson leave work early, cut down his work hours, and provide breaks for her from Gregory. Grayson complied but could not deal with Gregory. Soon, Gregory overwhelmed Grayson. In repeated tantrums, Gregory threw dishes, purposefully tossed or spilled food, and physically harmed the pets. One late afternoon, Gregory threw a milk glass into the television set. The screen exploded throwing glass across the living room.

Grace and Grayson began to quarrel. At first, the quarreling was loud arguments. Then it migrated to, Grace out of frustration, violently throwing objects at Grayson. Grayson moved out of the house which actually pleased Gregory. Grayson and Grace divorced when Gregory was twelve years old. Grace left Connecticut for California, knowing the California school system had many programs for disadvantaged children. One dreary wintery day, Grayson was fatally injured in a massive and fiery freeway wreck as he returned home from work. Grace nor Gregory attended his burial mass. They did not know of Grayson's demise. Grace called Connecticut social services in anger over not receiving her monthly support checks from Greg and was advised of his death. Her only response was, "What am I supposed to do now?"

Grace applied to every possible California and religious institution for financial assistance and was surprised at the support. The social support network in California provided better for Grace and Gregory than her previous support from Grayson.

Gregory continued to dominate Grace and outmaneuvered school personnel. He was devious, tricky, manipulative, and, at times, mean. Grace aged beyond her years but would not consider institutionalizing Gregory. Whenever such a thought even entered Grace's mind, Gregory would turn the tables on her and make it appear that Grace was the demented soul. Unexpectedly, Grace died when Gregory was about to turn sixteen. Grace collapsed with a brain hemorrhage while shopping for groceries. She lay paralyzed in the grocery store aisle until a stocker called for an ambulance. She was rushed to the hospital and put on life support. She struggled for life for another day and then appeared to give up. Gregory was found and brought to the hospital where he made tyrannical demands upon the doctors to "fix his mother."

They could not fix Grace.

The Social Services Department arranged for a welfare funeral for Grace. Gregory was the only attendee, and upon completion of the graveside service, he refused to let the cemetery workers lower the casket into the grave. It took three social service workers to restrain him. He broke loose as Grace's casket was lowered and miraculously hobbled to the grave site throwing himself into the grave.

Social Services was stuck with Gregory. They desperately wanted to be rid of him. The Social Services Department took his case before a judge. The judge simply reaffirmed the placement of Gregory into the care of the Social Services Department. He was assigned more social workers and a medical staff. Gregory's physical conditions made it difficult to place him in a foster home, but his behavior and attitude were an even larger deterrent. No one wanted Gregory. Gregory was placed in a specially supervised county-controlled living

Connecticut to California

facility and given special counseling. Social service workers referred to it as "the Greg house."

Part of Gregory's counseling was for psychological adjustment. Gregory liked the psychological sessions and behaved much better when in session. The other county counselors prefer Gregory spend most of his time away from them and with the psychologist. Gregory quickly learned to adjust his behavior to the person or party he was engaging. He could become very serious and pious in front of the clergy and also fit into a group watching a football game. Gregory was particularly good at fitting into discussions with women. Women did not find Gregory attractive or appealing. They seemed to enjoy his wit, his sarcasm, behind the back snide comments, bringing up others in their absence, and in general his gossipy nature.

Gregory was admitted to the university, given special treatment, and provided special accommodations. Social Services paid for his expenses, books, and tuition. Gregory excelled at academics but was failing socially which annoyed him. The handicapped and odd societal groups accepted Gregory. Gregory did not want to be part of these groups and in many ways was rude, mean, and inconsiderate to them. Gregory tried unsuccessfully to mingle with the mainstream student groups, popular groups, and jocks. They not only did not include Gregory, they avoided him. Gregory became an expert at football history, statistics, facts, and sports channel subject matter. Still the jocks slighted him. Gregory got the same results from the fraternity and sorority groups.

One day, while seated at the student union building drinking soda with a group of handicapped students, Gregory realized their group was not represented in campus politics. They were accommodated with many perks and benefits, but they were not included and accepted as an integral part of campus life and activity. For over a week, Gregory mulled his newfound realization. Strategically, he came to the conclusion that his physical appearance would publicly be a disadvantage. He decided it would be advantageous to have a more appealing handicapped person represent the causes. If he played his cards, selected the right person, he knew he could become the behind the scenes puppet master. Gregory laid the ground work for campus dissension regarding underrepresentation of handicapped students. He carefully studied who he might control and make beholding or grateful to him yet be a viable face for his political agendas. Gregory found Clara do be just the person for this role.

Gregory's next effort was to organize a petition to get more handicap ramps at the university. Clara was front and center for this cause. It was a smashing success. Within weeks, the university ground crews were installing ramps instead of working on other projects or manicuring the campus.

Gregory was delighted and found great excitement in his new ventures. He circulated another petition, demanding additional, closer, and more convenient handicap parking on campus. His campaign was successful, and Clara and the other handicap student were basking in the glory and attention garnered by Gregory's activities. Gregory enjoyed newfound fame and began to rethink the need for Clara as the front person.

Gregory then raised the issue that more males were on the student council than females. The point being, women were underrepresented, and there should be requirements for an equal number of women as men to represent the student body. Surprisingly, this effort stirred up heated debate concerning merit-based qualifications, ability to serve, and involvement in special interests areas. Gregory met with several sorority presidents. Most were very serious students. Gregory extolled the importance of democracy in America and on campus. His position was regardless of sex or gender, each person must have a vote. He emphasized that many female issues were ignored, not addressed, or even considered by the student council. Gregory focused on the absence of female athletic teams and available female intramural sports. He pointed out the exorbitant expense to the university in funding male sports teams and providing for male activities. Yet no offsetting female expenditures were being allocated. Gregory's insistent promotion led the sororities and women groups to throw their support to female candidates running for student council. Females soon outnumbered males in the student council.

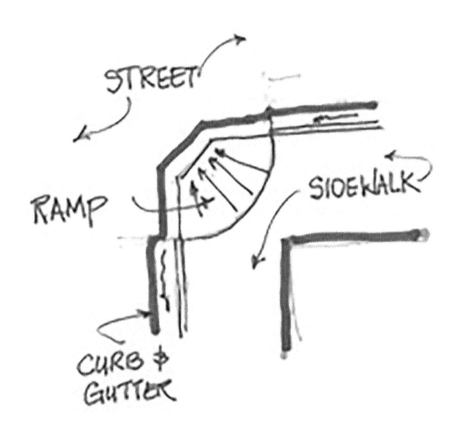

STREET

RAMP

SIDEWALK

CURB & GUTTER

Handicap Ramps

Then Gregory brought up the issue of underrepresentation of groups such as gays, lesbians, and minority races. He included the interest of handicapped individuals.

Although Gregory's studies had suffered somewhat due to his political activity, he was still an honor student. In his senior year, he was elected by a landslide to fill the newly created student senate position of chair for the disadvantaged. Gregory had a position on the Student Dias for Government, his own parking stall on campus, and a monthly opinion column in the student newspaper. Gregory loved his new status although his social life and female relationships still suffered.

During his final semester, Gregory interviewed for jobs as a CPA. He had passed his CPA examinations with excellent marks and threatened legal action if not awarded his certificate because he lacked the experience requirements. His arguments were legally weak, but the accountancy board feared his political activism as a handicap advocate and issued his license. Armed with his university transcripts, his CPA certificate, and what he felt was an exemplary resume, Gregory anticipated numerous and prestigious job offers. After the in-person interviews, no job offers came to Gregory. Gregory was angry and had to rely on everything the psychologists had taught him to control his behavior. Without medication, Gregory would break into uncontrollable outbursts when disturbed. He would direct bad behavior at anyone nearby, the world in general, and especially God. The campus psychiatrist prescribed medication to Gregory for behavioral control.

Gregory stayed near campus upon graduation and lived on his disability funds. From a rundown room in an apartment he shared with four other odd students, Gregory began to attend the student chapter of a major political party. Soon, Gregory realized he liked politics and recognized its vulnerability to manipulation. Gregory used his own funds to make posters depicting students running for office on campus from fraternity houses he disliked. He distorted their appearance, made allegations of their sexual persuasion, or created a history of violence for them. The posters were posted around campus. No one knew the source or author. Every student running for office that Gregory targeted and defamed was soundly defeated.

Campaign Signs

Gregory was amazed and deduced that his little campaign strategy was not only effective but lethal.

Gregory's made sure his reputation and successful tactics spread to the local politicians in his party that were seeking office. Four politicians were in difficult races. One of the well-funded candidates hired Gregory as his campaign treasurer. The money was equivalent to a part-time job, and Gregory loved the action. Getting paid was a bonus. He ordered all the statutes and laws on campaign finances, reporting, and soon became an expert in the field. He opened a variety of banking accounts to hold a variety of political contributions. The other three candidates soon hired Gregory as their paid campaign treasures. Gregory now virtually had a full-time paying job. He used his CPA background to file reports, shift funds, shield donations, and obfuscate contributors.

Gregory helped strategize the candidates' campaigns and platforms, did opposition research against their opponents, and laundered sizable campaign contributions into various accounts. The candidates focused on fund-raising and campaign appearances. All four candidates that Gregory worked for were victorious. Gregory at times would angrily disagree with his candidates over strategy or approach. With his medication and psychological anger management training, he maintained his composure.

Gregory began to use the name Greg. He thought it's more mature. With his newfound fame as a political operative, he landed a job in the valley as an accountant in a legal firm that performed tax work and estate planning and severed as counsel to several cities. The firm made numerous political contributions to candidates in both parties, but by far the largest donations were to the party controlling political power. Greg accepted the position as assistant central party chairman for the four largest counties. Greg negotiated with his employer and the party hierarchy to keep his job as treasurer for several politicians. Greg was owed considerable favors from these politicians. He was well reimbursed for his services from their campaign funds. Greg was not only a powerful politically operator, he was becoming wealthy.

Judith Elizabeth O'leery was a physically overdeveloped young lady with a below average face. She was named after her mother and grandmother. To eliminate some of the name confusion, she went by the name Elizabeth. She was moderately popular in her large parochial high school class. More noticeably, she was a favorite of the priests and nuns of the dioceses. In her senior year, she asked the high school quarterback to the Sadie Hawkins dance. Before the night was over, Elizabeth found herself in the cafeteria parking lot in the back seat of the quarterback's car. They had sex. This activity became a regular occurrence after home football games.

Elizabeth became pregnant.

The nuns made arrangements for Elizabeth to attend a special school in another diocese and have her baby. The quarterback's parents also attended Elizabeth's church and became aware of her circumstance and their son's involvement. They visited Elizabeth monthly and began to insist their son accept his responsibilities. Elizabeth and Jordan were married. They lived in the small town, and by the time Elizabeth was twenty-five, she had four children. Elizabeth's life was busy, and Jordan was unfaithful. They divorced, and Elizabeth, with the help of the church, moved to another town.

She met Taylor in church. He was a real estate salesman, and after six months of dating, they were married. Over the next eight years, Elizabeth had five more children. Elizabeth's life was extremely busy, and Taylor was unfaithful. Elizabeth was distraught. To move forward with her life, she enrolled in evening classes at the local community college. She obtained an AA certificate, and as the children were more involved in their school activities, she landed a part-time bookkeeping job. Taylor and Elizabeth divorced when she was forty-three years old. Elizabeth met with her priest for advice and direction. They prayed, and with the help of the church, Elizabeth moved to the valley and landed an office job in the same firm that employed Greg.

Being the kind, gentle, religious, and caring person she was, Elizabeth took pity upon Greg, his dilapidated physical condition, his appearance, and absence from a normal social life. When she baked, she always brought him cookies and cakes. She would shop for him at the local grocery and drugstores. She delivered his goods to his house and stocked his pantry. Most importantly, she picked up his various pills and prescriptions at the local pharmacy. Greg was inconsistent in taking his medication regiment of pills for his various ailments. Daily at work, Elizabeth made sure Greg took his pills. She even fetched water for him. Greg came to rely on Elizabeth and gave her keys to his house and car.

The town pharmacist was a slight built, nonathletic, homely, and frail man named Ralph. It so happened Ralph grew up in the same town as Elizabeth and occasionally attended the same church. In fact, Ralph was in the same class as Elizabeth in high school. Elizabeth did not recognize nor remember Ralph. He was not on the football team. But Ralph remembered Elizabeth.

Elizabeth was now forty-nine years old, and her last child was in her last year of high school. She was forty pounds overweight but still had a feminine figure. Her face had not improved, and Elizabeth did little to make herself attractive. Elizabeth had managed financially with her child support payments, some alimony payments, her paltry salary, help from her parents, and help from the church. Elizabeth was not attracted to Ralph, but they began to have dinner occasionally, and he asked her to go to the movies often. Greg did not like Elizabeth sharing time with Ralph. When Elizabeth's last daughter graduated high school, Elizabeth consented to one of Ralph's numerous proposals. They were married in the local church by Elizabeth's favorite priest.

At work, Greg began to encourage Elizabeth to run for elected office. In fact, Greg pestered and nagged Elizabeth to become politically involved. Greg could maneuver Elizabeth, and she needed his continual guidance to avoid trouble with her error-ridden work. A vacancy arose on the school board. With Greg's input, Elizabeth decided to go by Judith, her given first name. Her mother and grandmother had died, and there no longer was a concern for name confusion. Four other candidates were competing for the school board position, but Greg told Judith he knew how to handle and outmaneuver them. Unbeknownst to the other candidates, Greg cleverly defined them to the electorate as having serious character issues

Community College

regarding behavior, past infidelities, indiscretions, and inaccurate or false resumes. None of these accusations were true. Judith won handily.

As a school board member, for the first time in Judith's life, she was an important person politically and socially. Her lunches and dinners were miraculously paid for. She was invited to numerous wine parties and outings all paid for by others. Ralph was a home body, and Judith truly enjoyed her popularity.

With a year remaining on her school board term, the position of commissioner was up for election. Although a part-time position, the commissioner position paid a handsome salary with benefits. Greg encouraged Judith to seek the office. Once again, Greg would handle the campaign. The firm Judith worked for indicated if she won the commissioner position, they would pay her the same salary, but she could work part-time, at her leisure. Judith, under the guidance and management of Greg, once again handily won the election. With two elected positions, her part-time job, helping Greg with his medications and groceries, and attending numerous parties and functions, Judith was busy. Judith lost twenty pounds, dressed better, and decided to be known simply as Liz.

Liz loved her new lifestyle and was even more important. She was invited and went on several junkets paid for by lobbyists. She truly enjoyed the attention of men much more interesting, powerful, successful, and handsome than Ralph. Ralph was content behind his pill counter and watching sports on television at home. In fact, Liz and Ralph's relationship was severely lacking. On an out of town trip, Liz spent dinner and the evening with a young lobbyist. She was twitterpated by his attentiveness. She accompanied him to his room and stayed the night. Liz became social and intimate with several lobbyists and businessmen in the state. Most of the men were married and had families. Liz and Ralph attended mass with them and their families. Liz weekly went to confession but only confessed things she felt her priest would be comfortable hearing.

Greg was aging. The doctors had always told Greg his life expectancy would be less than normal. How much less was never discussed, but Greg was in his midfifties. The numerous medications

Greg took were hard on his less than perfect organs. One pill which Greg used for anxiety was particularly hard on his liver, kidneys, and heart. The dosage had to be purposefully kept small. The medication could dangerously build up, causing his organs to malfunction or completely shut down. Greg relied on the medication because it quieted his nerves, made him less excitable, and greatly calmed his anger urges. The pill was Exasitol. It was very expensive.

The central committee chairmanship was opening in the coming year. Greg wanted the position badly. Some prominent politicians liked the work Greg performed and the results he obtained, but they thought his appearance needed to be kept behind the scenes. Most thought Liz a better choice for the position. This situation put Liz and Greg into an awkward relationship. Yet they both insisted they would support one another.

Greg's character and modus operandi did not change. He purposefully and clandestinely leaked false information that Liz had discretionary issues that if exposed to the electorate would damage the parties' reputation. The lobbyists let it be known to Liz what Greg was up to. They preferred Liz win the chairmanship but, at the same time, were afraid of Greg and what he might do. They resented Greg extorting large contributions from them, which they paid. They knew they could not completely trust Greg. This situation was unsettling and troubling to many of the local and state party members.

One evening, when Liz was attending a function, socializing, rubbing political elbows, and consuming free wine, she decided to go by the pharmacy where Ralph was holding down the evening shift. She asked Ralph to refill Greg's Exasitol prescription with a much stronger dosage. She explained to Ralph that Greg was overly anxious and could not sleep. Ralph cautioned Liz of the danger of a high dosage and said, "Once Greg takes these pills, he will continually want them because of their feeling of instant relief. They can become immediately addictive."

Liz smiled demurely at Ralph and replied, "Ralph, Greg is well aware of the risk of this medication. He has been taking it for years."

Ralph provided Liz with the stronger Exasitol.

The following day at work, Liz accompanied Greg to lunch. They discussed the power, financial rewards, and prestige of holding the chairmanship position. Liz conceded the position could be ideal for Greg since he could function behind the scenes. Greg told Liz another national party position would open next cycle, and he would be glad to support her for that position.

Liz said, "Greg, I know I can trust you and you would protect my reputation. I am going to withdraw from the chairman consideration. I want you to have that position."

Greg was taken back. He knew the lobbyists wanted Liz as chairman, and he had already strategically positioned innuendo, half-truths, and slanderous information in place to defeat Liz. In fact, the attack on Liz may end her political career completely.

Greg was taken back. He softly and very quietly said, "Thank you, Liz. I am grateful for your kind consideration of me. I…I…I… don't really know what to say, except thank you."

For the first time in his life, Greg was humble. His thoughts migrated back to his mother, Grace, and he lowered eyes and guard toward Liz. Uncharacteristically, Greg became conciliatory toward another person.

Greg continued, "Liz, this is a relief. But to be honest, the best chance for party support and funding for a national office for you is if you were the central committee chairman."

Liz responded, "Hmm? Well, maybe I should reconsider? Would you mind, Greg?"

Greg said, "Well, I do want the chairman's position. You know I am much better at all that campaigning and election stuff than you are."

Greg felt himself becoming very angry. His guarded and bombastic self returned. He thought himself stupid for giving Liz the slightest opening. His face flushed red, he could feel his pulse, and his heart raced. He reached to his pocket for his Exasitol pills. He said, "Damn, I forgot my pills."

Liz responded, "Oh, I picked up your prescription yesterday."

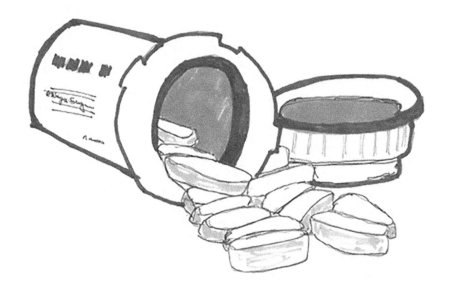

Gregory's Pills

She handed Greg the pill bottle. Greg reached for a glass of water and took a pill. Almost immediately, his heart rate dropped, and he felt the flushing leave his face.

Greg said, "Oh that is much better. In fact I feel great. Liz, let's work out an arrangement for both of us over this chairman's job."

Liz responded, "Greg, you know I have always helped you, and I want to help you now. But based on what you just said and since I have told the lobbyists I would seek the job, I think I should pursue it."

Greg's face turned red again, and his pulse quickened. He reached for the water and took another pill. He took a deep breath and waited a few minutes and then said, "I understand, Liz, but I can handle the lobbyists, and besides, I know you have many indiscretions that could come out and damage your marriage and hurt your political future."

Liz was shaken by his comments. She retorted, "Greg, are you threatening me? Surely, you realize I work where you do, and I know all about your money shuffling and funding maneuvers."

Greg's heart was racing, and again, he reached for the water and took another pill. He sat back, relaxed, and slurped up some spaghetti. Greg loved spaghetti. Then he calmly said, "Liz, I think we should all have a meeting away from the valley and search out a strategy for the party and each of us. Would you go for that?"

Liz replied, "Greg, I will always try to be open and fair. I have always helped and stood by you. You know I am a very religious person and have always tried to do the right thing. My problem is I have already given my word and accepted money from the businessmen and lobbying groups."

Once again, Greg reached for the water and took another pill. Greg and Liz finished their lunch in silence. They cordially separated, and Greg went back to the office and Liz attended a political meeting and had several glasses of free wine.

Liz was troubled about Greg. On the way home that evening, she rendezvoused with one of the lobbyists at a local expensive restaurant. Over dinner and wine, she explained the issues that arose at lunch. They discussed potential strategies, finished dinner, and in the parking lot decided to climb into the back seat of his Mercedes to work out a plan.

The next day, Greg was absent from work. Greg never missed work; it was his life. At noon, Liz went to his home. She knocked on the door. There was no answer. She impatiently waited and knocked again. Still, there was no answer. She dug in her purse and found his house keys and entered the house. Greg was at the kitchen table, slumped over into a plate of cold spaghetti. She felt for his pulse. There was none. Greg was cold and stiff. Greg was dead.

Liz picked up the Exasitol bottle next to his plate. It was empty. She put the pill bottle in her purse, removed her cell phone, and called the police. Liz silently waited until the coroner arrived.

After a cursory review of the premises and Greg's condition, the coroner stated, "This is of natural causes. There will be no investigation."

He told Liz she was free to leave. She left and aimlessly drove around town for nearly an hour. Her mind was surprisingly calm and composed, as she contemplated her feelings. She reached the conclusion she was tired of being pushed around. She did not deserve her treatment at the hands of Jordan or Taylor. They were lying and cheating bums. Liz had raised the children. She was the responsible one who carried the parental burdens of children and worried about their well-being and welfare. Greg was also abusive to her. He used her and continually made demands on her time. Greg was self-centered and manipulative.

Liz knew Ralph had worn her down with his numerous proposals. She asked herself, "Why did I settle for him?"

She was not happy about her decisions and wondered why she did not have higher self-esteem and personal worth. She would live with Ralph as long as he stayed out of her personal lifestyle and made no demands on her or her time.

With little awareness, Liz found herself in front of her church. She turned off the car ignition and went in. She placed a dollar in the collection box and took an altar candle. She lit the candle, went to the altar, and knelt. She said a prayer to God, asking for help and guidance as she moved forward in life.

Spaghetti

Slowly driving home to Ralph, Liz wondered, *Who will take care of Greg's estate?* She knew he had to be wealthy, and he had no living relatives.

She thought, *Surely, with all the estate planning he did for others, he must have a will. His will and papers were probably at his house.* She reached across the car seat and fumbled in her purse, making sure she still had his house keys.

> *"For brothers, you have been given freedom, not freedom to do wrong, but freedom to love and serve each other." (Galatians. 5:13)*

> *"Be watchful, the Devil prowls around like a roaring lion, seeking someone to devour." (I Peter 5:8)*

Jerry Hanson. 2018

Church

About the Author

J erry Hanson lived and led an unassuming but delightful life as a country kid. He never knew he was a country kid until he went to school in the city. In the city, everything and everyone was measuring and assuming. Socially surviving under new standards, Jerry distanced himself from his country friends. The country kids were his true friends. Matriculating in difficult curricula, he survived the rigors of higher education. He served his country honorably and entered the private work world. Once again, he encountered a competitive and comparative culture. Throughout his life, Jerry has owned a professional firm, developed property, owned a company, and held several prestige positions. He never endeavored to become an author.

Even during hectic times, Jerry observed and marveled at the world and its inhabitants. He finds people the most interesting, intriguing, yet confusing. Their individual backgrounds, morals, ethics, logic, and skills or lack thereof are unique, complex, and amazing. Jerry does not consider himself an intellect. He simply has some thoughts, insights, and observations to share in short stories. These twelve short stories are meant to be enjoyed while tickling your conscience regarding values and virtues.

Jerry's greatest accomplishment was his wife marrying him. Together they raised a wonderful son and daughter. Any parent worth their salt will face reality raising children. Even more sobering is observing your children raising their children. Values, morals, and ethics will become obvious. The foundations for their character were laid yesterday by your character. The results stand before you.

There is another day of reckoning coming, and maybe one of Jerry's short stories will ignite a glimmer of observation about yourself, the world you live in, and your value system. These short stories make a wonderful and economical gift to friends or associates. Good reading to you.

CPSIA information can be obtained
at www.ICGtesting.com
Printed in the USA
LVHW010850110820
662878LV00002B/161